SURVIVE THE FALL BOOK TWO

MADNESS RISING

D1607438

DEREK SHUPERT

ALSO BY DEREK SHUPERT

SURVIVE THE FALL SERIES:
POWERLESS WORLD
MADNESS RISING
DARK ROADS

THE COMPLETE DEAD STATE SERIES:
DEAD STATE: CATALYST (PREQUEL)
DEAD STATE: FALLOUT
DEAD STATE: SURVIVAL ROAD
DEAD STATE: EXECUTIONER
DEAD STATE: IMMUNE
DEAD STATE: EVOLVED

THE COMPLETE DEAD STATE SERIES BOX SET

THE COMPLETE AFFLICTED SERIES:
GENESIS (PREQUEL)
PATIENT ZERO
RIPTIDE
DEAD RECKONING

THE HUNTRESS BANE SERIES:
THE HUNTRESS BANE (SHORT STORY)
TAINTED HUNTER
CRIMSON THIRST

THE COMPLETE BALLISTIC MECH SERIES:
DIVISION
INFERNO
EXTINCTION
PAYBACK

STAND ALONE
SENTRY SQUAD

DEDICATION

I wouldn't be able to write without those who support me. I thank you for your encouragement and being there for me.

To those that read my books, I thank you for your support.

CHAPTER ONE

RUSSELL

Russell kept the gas pedal pressed to the floorboard of the Explorer. He pushed the battered SUV along the winding roads that sliced through the Blue Ridge Mountains at near reckless speeds. Dense forests lined the sides of the two-lane roadway—a solid wall with no opening or gap within the rich vegetation.

The large off-road tires squealed as they hugged the turns. Russell eased off the gas some, but not much.

He was shaken and wanted nothing more than to get to the Luray sheriff's station as fast as he could. Time wasn't on their side.

The encounter with Marcus Wright's men had rattled him, and it showed. The band of thugs had swarmed the log home with guns blazing, trying to silence all that were inside.

Russell took deep, hard breaths to try and stay his nerves. It did little good.

His pulse spiked. Beads of sweat populated his brow and ran down the sides of his flushed, dingy face in streaks.

He checked the rearview mirror, but couldn't see past the large dogs milling about in the rear of the Explorer. Both Max and Butch watched the road, snarling and huffing. They glanced over the back seat, and barked a warning.

Thomas Kinkade, Cathy's dear friend, laid slumped in the seat behind him.

Cathy Snider, the prepper and survivalist who saved him from the clutches of a ravenous mountain lion, checked the passenger side view mirror for any incoming threats. Her rifle sat between her legs. She wrapped her fingers around the barrel with a firm grasp as she breathed heavily from her nose.

"I'm not seeing any other trucks or what not coming up on us. I think we're ok for now, but keep your eyes peeled," she said.

"Do you think they gave up?" Russell dipped his chin and peered through the driver's side view mirror.

Cathy shrugged. "Doubtful, but I guess we'll see. Doesn't really matter if they have or not. We just need to get to the sheriff's station pronto."

Smoke plumed into the sky behind the battered SUV. Trails of gray reached above the tree line from where the red Chevy Dually had skirted past the Explorer and crashed earlier.

The steering wheel vibrated in Russell's firm grip. There was plenty of feedback coming from the front end of the Explorer. Something had been jarred loose or damaged when the Dually had rammed the vehicle and tried to run them off the road.

Russell pumped the brake, slowing the Explorer as they hit a winding curve that took them along the edge of a steep drop off.

"Can't be sure, but I think we have a problem here," Russell said, as he fought to keep the SUV from drifting into the guardrail.

Cathy cut away from the side view mirror and looked at Russell. "What's the issue?"

"There's a ton of vibration in the steering wheel. Feels like the front end might be messed up. I don't know."

Thomas groaned from the back seat as he leaned forward. His hand was pressed to the gunshot wound he sustained when they fled his house. A stray bullet had caught his arm.

"How is it?" Cathy asked. "Move your hand so I can get a better look at it."

"Stings like a bitch, but it's not too bad," Thomas said, shifting his weight to the side.

"I'll be the judge of how bad it is." Cathy twisted in her seat, then reached toward his injured arm. She moved the pieces of torn fabric out of the way, so she could get a better idea of the damage.

Russell peered into the rearview mirror and craned his neck, watching Cathy remove the bloody pieces of clothing from the wound.

Cathy studied the gunshot wound. "It doesn't look too bad, a graze that caught the meat of your arm. Should be able to get it dressed once we reach the sheriff's station. Just keep pressure on it until we get there."

Thomas cocked his head, then dipped his chin to inspect the flesh. He maneuvered his arm and placed his fingers around the tattered skin. "Been some time since I've been shot. Hasn't been since Vietnam, I think. Caught a round in my lower thigh. Back then, though, I was able to take it better, being young and all."

Cathy smirked. "I bet you were just as stubborn back then as what you are now. Charging into bad situations without thinking things through. You're lucky you were just grazed. That bullet could've caught a vital organ or worse yet, killed you right then and there. Next time, think before you act, ok?"

The SUV hit a straightaway. Russell turned in his seat and peered over his shoulder. "I agree with Cathy, but I understand why you charged the front door. A man has to defend his household against any threats."

"Don't encourage him," Cathy said, while rolling her eyes. "There's a difference between defending oneself and being foolish. It's a thin red line that can blur and be crossed before you know it. Case in point. If the shit hits the fan, you do the smart thing to survive."

"Regardless, I'm just glad you're ok and that it's not too bad." Russell faced forward and spotted a street sign with Luray written in bold, white letters and an arrow pointing in the direction they were heading. He caught sight of the town just above the tree line in the distance. Safety was close at hand.

Cathy flicked her wrist, motioning for Thomas to sit back. "Keep pressure on it. If you have something to tie it off with, that would be good too."

Thomas deflated against the seat without so much as a single word in protest.

Butch, his large, black cane corso, leaned over the seat and licked the side of Thomas's face. Max, Cathy's black and brown German shepherd, flicked his tongue at his other cheek.

Cathy snapped her fingers, then pointed at Max. "Leave him be. You'll be able to love on him later."

Thomas pointed at the dash with a trembling finger. "They might have damaged an axle or something. For sure feels like the alignment is off."

Russell cut his gaze to the rearview mirror and asked, "How can you tell?"

Madness Rising

"I've had this SUV for a long time and have worked on various parts ad nauseam. To say that I have grown intimate with every inch of this brute is an understatement."

"Like I said, it doesn't matter what it is as long as we make it to the station in one piece," Cathy said. "That's what we need to focus on. After we get there, then we can address the vehicle."

Russell pumped the brake, then jerked the steering wheel hard to the right. The SUV swerved around a minivan that was stopping at the sign. Cars from both directions blared their horns in protest as they slammed their brakes.

"Whoa," Russell muttered under his breath. He made a wide arch to the highway heading east into town.

Cathy braced her hands against the dash and window as gravity forced her against the passenger door. "Let's not kill us before we get there. All right, Cage?"

The clanging noise from the Explorer grew louder as he straightened the SUV out.

"I'm the least of your worries," he shot back. "Besides, we all have places we need to be. I'm just trying to save us time, is all."

"Yeah, well, again, you'll be no use to your wife if you're dead or so banged up that you can't travel. I'd like to see my daughter too." Cathy removed her hands from the dash, then pointed at the town dead ahead. "Luray is coming up. Not much farther to the sheriff's station."

Russell tilted his head, but didn't comment. His main, if not only priority, was getting to his wife, Sarah, any way he could. At the moment, that was his mission, and the only purpose he had in his life.

The grinding of metal filled the cab of the Explorer as the steering wheel rattled in Russell's hands. He eased off the gas, but kept their speed running at a decent clip.

The lights at the approaching intersection were dead. No bright colors shone from the signal's plastic lens. It was a strange feeling running through the lights with no indication of what should be done. He checked both ways at the intersection to avoid another tongue lashing or accident.

Russell thought the lights would at least flash red or even yellow, to indicate there was an issue somewhere along the line. Then again, if the grid had been taken out, would they even flash?

The Explorer plowed through two more intersections. He checked each side of the road with a quick glance that found no cars approaching.

Russell eyed the gauges on the dash while flitting his gaze to the road ahead of them for any traffic or other obstacles that could be in their way.

No warnings flashed from the dash, but Russell figured with the issues plaguing the aging vehicle there wouldn't be any indictor to warn what the exact ailment was.

One issue at a time. Not everything can be resolved all at once.

Russell's stomach twisted in knots. Every grind of tortured metal from the Explorer made him feel as though he was that much further away from getting to Sarah, in Boston. Patience and faith were what he had to rely on, but that was easier said than done.

"Well, something big has happened. That's for damn sure," Cathy said, while staring out of the windshield. "There's normally more traffic heading into downtown than this. Folks might be hesitant about getting out and are just staying home. Might be waiting things out. I know a number of folks up here use HAM radios. They might be working right now. Can't be sure, though. Either way, I'm glad they're not on the roads."

Russell followed the curve of the road into Luray. The aged reddish-brown brick buildings concealed the street beyond the structures. Russell craned his neck while working the brake and gas in tandem.

Cathy pointed out the windshield, then glanced over to him. "The sheriff's station isn't much farther. When you come to Plainview, hook a right. We've still got a few blocks to go before we get there, though."

A handful of cars were parked along the sidewalks next to the windowless buildings. More traffic signals and crosswalk indicators were void of any power.

Shops that lined the streets were dark and vacant. A handful of young people milled about the fronts of the shops, peering through the windows to the dark interiors.

The teenage kids looked suspect at best which made Russell wonder if they were scoping out places to break into.

"Maybe the sheriff will know what has happened, or at least, give us some insight as to what might be going on," Russell said.

"That's a big if, but I wouldn't hold my breath," Cathy replied with a snide tone. "He's a joke. Laughable at best. I wish we had another option, but he's all we've got at the moment." The hate she felt for the man clung to each word that she breathed into existence.

Russell turned toward her. Her face twisted in horror, and she pointed out the driver's side window. "Watch out!"

He looked back to the driver's side window.

A black, extended cab truck plowed through the intersection at full speed.

Russell caught a brief glimpse of the masked occupants in the truck before they struck the Explorer, wondering how they could have found them.

The crunching of metal plagued the interior of the cab. The driver's side window cracked as the side of Russell's head slammed into the glass.

Airbags deployed, exploding from the steering column and dash like shotgun blasts. The puffy white bags punched them in the face. The seat belts cinched down around their waists and across their chests.

The SUV lumbered across the intersection and crashed into a yellow hatchback.

The bellowing of the horn screeched. Smoke venting from the engine filled the cab as they stirred.

Grumbles of discomfort and confusion fled the lips of the occupants. Both Max and Butch groaned from the rear of the SUV, then barked as the seconds ticked by.

Russell squinted his eyes, trying to squash the festering pain that stabbed his body. Nothing felt broken, just battered from the collision.

A dull, throbbing pain pounded through his head.

Disorientation clung to him like a leech.

He licked his dry, coarse lips, then asked, "Is everyone... all right?"

CHAPTER TWO

RUSSELL

Cathy grimaced, then winced. She leaned away from the deflated airbag. Wiry strands of her golden locks stuck out from the sides of her scalp. A groan emitted from her mouth. She reached for the seat belt latch, slow and unsure.

"Yeah. I think I'm all right," she answered in a weak tone.

Russell tilted his head clockwise toward the back of the SUV. The motion hurt. The strained muscles in his neck ached. The pain dialed up the farther he turned his head.

Thomas was sprawled out in the backseat and slumped over on his side. His skeletal fingers clutched his wounded arm. The wiry strands of gray hair poked out from his eyebrows. A thin string of blood trickled down from the side of his mouth, discoloring the gray stubble on his chin. A thick, wide gash snaked along his forehead, and his eyes were clamped shut.

"Thomas, can you hear me?" Russell asked.

9

A groan fled the elderly man's thin lips. His face contorted as he squeezed his eyes shut.

"Good man," Russell said.

Both dogs barked and growled from the rear of the Explorer. They seemed to be all right from what Russell could see in the rearview mirror and what he heard from the agitated canines.

"Come on, we need to—" Russell tugged on his seat belt but stopped when the back driver's side door creaked open.

An arm stretched out over Thomas's body as the dogs growled and snapped at the limb.

"Christ," a muffled voice yelled. The mysterious man withdrew from the cab in a blink.

Thomas stirred in the seat.

Russell glanced through the spider webbed driver's side window to the side view mirror. A figure loomed just beyond the Explorer with a weapon shouldered and the barrel trained at the SUV. His vision was foggy and coated with a haze that made it difficult to see who it was and what they were doing. Although, he had his suspicions.

The passenger side door wrenched open next to Cathy. A masked man stood with a pistol drawn and trained at the cab. The crackling of static and chatter loomed from the two-way radio on the masked man's hip. The voice on the other end was choppy and hard to make out.

The masked man pulled the radio from his belt, then said, "I got them coming into Luray, over."

Static–

"Copy that."

The masked man's intense gaze narrowed at Russell through the open slits in the dingy black mask before shifting to Cathy.

"Come over here, and give me a hand, will ya?" he said, snapping at his partner.

Madness Rising

"Those damn mutts almost took my arm off." The other man pointed at the barking dogs from the open door.

"Stop being a pussy and get over here," his cohort demanded. "We don't want to hang around any longer than we need to. The clock's ticking."

"What about the old man? Aren't we taking both?"

"Change of plans. We're just here for her. Now come on."

"I'm not going anywhere with you," Cathy snarled. Her voice was laced with contempt. She reached for the rifle between her legs.

The masked man struck the side of her head with the back of his hand. A yelp of pain spewed from her lips as her head snapped to the side.

Russell grit his teeth and jerked at the seat belt.

The masked man trained the pistol at Russell's skull. "Don't do anything stupid there, cowboy, unless you want a slug to the head."

Max leaned over the backseat, bearing his fangs and growling at the vile men.

The masked man pressed the barrel of the pistol to her temple as she sat upright in the seat. He reached between her legs, grabbed the rifle, then handed it to his partner. "Undo the seat belt, now, and step out."

Cathy thumbed the release button, but the latch wouldn't come free. "I can't. It's jammed or something."

Russell kept his hands on the steering wheel, watching the men and Cathy like a hawk.

Thomas was silent in the back seat.

The masked man's partner slapped his chest. "I hear sirens. Plus, we've got eyes on us. We need to jet."

"We're not leaving without her," he said, raising his voice an octave higher.

He shoved the gun in the waistband of his smirched jeans, then pulled his blade from the sheath on his hip.

The blade slipped between the belt and Cathy's torso. He sliced through the restraint with ease.

Max surged over the far backseat with his front paws resting on the seat before Thomas's body. His ears folded back. He snapped at the men with glistening fangs.

The masked man yanked Cathy from her seat by her arm, then dragged her out of the SUV.

The trio skirted the rear of the Explorer toward the truck that flanked them.

Max finished crawling over the seat and bolted from the SUV, barking and growling at the masked men.

Butch stayed and licked at Thomas's face.

Russell fumbled with his seat belt, jerking and tugging at the strap. It clicked free from the housing. He flung the belt to the side. The metal tip clanged off the cracked window.

His Glock. It wasn't in his lap anymore.

"What's going–on?" Thomas asked as he slowly sat up.

In a panic, Russell grabbed the handle to the door and pulled, but it didn't budge. He threw his shoulder into the bent door twice, pushing it out from the vehicle an inch.

The engine from the truck revved. He was running out of time.

"Where's Cathy?" Thomas asked with a confused looked on his face.

Russell forced the door open farther and stepped out. A wave of weakness attacked his legs, and sent him crumbling to his knees.

Max clawed at the driver's side of the truck as its engine roared.

Madness Rising

Russell turned to the cab and peered at the floorboard. The Glock was nestled in the far corner. Must have slipped from his lap when they crashed.

He grabbed the piece and stood up.

The world swayed.

The ground rushed toward him.

He stumbled a bit, trying to keep upright.

Both hands pressed against Russell's head as he fought through the dizziness.

The truck tore ass in reverse and peeled away from the wreckage with Max running next to the vehicle.

Russell cracked open his eyes and stumbled forward. He brought the Glock to bear at the fleeing truck, but struggled to get a clear shot.

He squinted his eyes, then opened them wide. He popped off a single round that pinged off the passenger side fender of the truck.

The pickup flung around in one fluid motion as Russell pursued into the intersection.

Brake lights flashed, then vanished as the rear tires spun wildly.

The blaring sirens of help loomed large from behind Russell.

Focusing on the truck, Russell placed both hands on the grip of the Glock to steady his trembling arms. He lined up his shot as best he could. It was now or nothing. His final chance.

Sweat stung his eyes. His finger caressed the trigger as screeching tires and flashing lights flanked him in the intersection.

The driver's side door of the vehicle that pulled up on the Explorer flew open. A burly, heavyset man stepped out and drew his pistol.

"Drop the gun, now." His voice boomed like angry thunder.

Russell kept the Glock fixed at the truck that vanished down a side street. He managed to read the first few letters of the license.

"Boy, I'm not going to tell you again. Drop your weapon, and place your hands on the back of your head."

Russell lowered the Glock, then set it down on the road. He placed his hands on the back of his head and stood still.

The heavyset sheriff moved around the front of his black and tan Prowler. The barrel of his sidearm trained at Russell's head as he closed the distance. He grabbed Russell's wrists and yanked them down to his waist.

"I'm not sure what went on here, but we don't tolerate people discharging weapons in the-" He paused as Max ran up to Russell. "Isn't that Cathy Snider's dog?"

"It is. She was taken a few seconds ago by some masked men in a pickup truck. That's who I was firing at," Russell answered.

The teenagers loitering about in front of the nearby shops had all vanished.

The sheriff finished cuffing Russell, then spun him around. He looked to the SUV. Thomas emerged from the backseat. Blood trickled down from the gash above his brow.

"I think you have some explaining to do here, son."

CHAPTER THREE

SARAH

Adrenaline spiked through Sarah's veins. The surge made her lightheaded and a bit dizzy. The tips of her fingers tingled with fright. The muscles in her legs burned with each stride. She panted, trying to fill her lungs with oxygen that was spent in a blink.

Kinnerk's henchmen were hot on their trail, and closing in fast. Sarah could hear their bulk behind her. Their footfalls hammered the concrete of the sidewalk. Threats were shouted from the vile men who added ample incentive to keep moving.

The goons had caught up to them through the rising madness that had laid siege to the city. They were relentless and held fast in taking them down.

Rick, Sarah's new ally, ditched his car a few blocks back and hoofed it on foot. A traffic jam had stifled their progress in getting to Sarah's friend's place on the other side of Boston and away from the unscrupulous thugs.

It was a misunderstanding that trapped her and Rick into a dangerous situation, and complicated her life even more.

The henchmen were looking for Allen, the owner of the automotive shop where Rick's car had been kept. He had a debt that was owed and had vanished from the mob boss's radar. His men had come to collect, and Rick and Sarah happened to be in the wrong place at the wrong time. Despite any pleas made to the men in tow, her words fell on deaf ears.

Rick was done trying to convince the thugs that they knew nothing about Kinnerk's money, or where Allen had gone. They had a job to complete, and needed answers. Rick and Sarah were their only lead.

"Here," Rick shouted through each hard breath that fled his lips. "Don't slow down. We've got to keep moving and give them the slip."

That was easier said than done. At least for Rick, it was. Sarah was in decent shape, but the punishment she had waged on her body the last few days, and the lack of sleep and proper nutrition, were catching up to her fast.

Her energy levels waned and dropped with each hard step she took. She battled through the pain that ravaged her legs and lungs. Both were on fire and stung with each second that ticked by. It wasn't a time to give up, though. Their life hung in the balance.

Rick skirted the edge of the drab building they were running alongside. The derelict structure had seen better days.

The exterior had signs of wear and tear that made it look unstable. The reddish-brown acme brick was chipped and scored with portions of the dense pressed clay crumbling in spots.

Trash littered the sidewalks. Ash rained down like snow during the winter solstice and tickled Sarah's face.

Madness Rising

Fires that ravaged the metropolis pumped large swathes of black smoke and other debris into the sky. Boston looked more like hell on earth now than anything else.

A crackle of gunfire caused Sarah to flinch and gasp. Her heart skipped a beat. The buzzing of the incoming round flanked her as she hooked the corner of the dilapidated building. The bullet chipped away at the brick as she vanished from the henchmen's sight.

Tiny fragments of clay fluttered in the air in her wake as she breathed a sigh of relief. It was another close call that she had avoided. Though, she wasn't out of the woods yet.

"You ok?" Rick asked, inclining his head.

His damp shirt clung to his slender, muscular frame. Beads of sweat raced the length of his neck and vanished under the collar. His hair bounced with every step he made.

"Barely. They're shooting at us." Sarah stumbled down the passageway. Her legs wanted to give out, but the henchmen hadn't given up and neither could she. Her best friend, Mandy, and, husband, Russell, filled her thoughts. She didn't know if they were all right or where they were for that matter. The unknown kept her going.

Like a stallion running full tilt, Rick pulled away from Sarah. He peered over his shoulder, and his pace lessened. He skimmed over the buildings that had them trapped on either side. Making it to the other end of the alley wasn't going to happen with the goons keeping within striking distance. There had to be an entrance somewhere they could slip through.

Sarah caught up to Rick as he looked over the sprawling exterior, searching for a way inside. She huffed and deflated against the wall. Her chest pulsated in and out as she struggled to catch her breath.

The clamoring of the henchmen was just beyond the corner of the building which sent a wave of terror flooding her body. Sarah grabbed her Glock 43 from her waistband. She chambered a round as she fought to steady her trembling hands.

Rick whistled, capturing Sarah's focus.

She looked away from the Glock. He had moved down to the other side of a roll off dumpster that was overflowing with debris. He pointed to the building behind her, then disappeared alongside the immense dumpster.

What the hell?

Sarah took a step back. She stooped down and peered through the narrow opening between the roll off and the building.

The henchmen crested the passageway. Raised Irish voices spoke with anger.

A stack of crates that sat off to her side facing the thugs concealed her whereabouts, for now. She stayed low and entered the passageway.

Rick materialized at the other end, waving his hand in a frantic manner. The smell of the trash and waste invaded her nose. It grew worse by the middle of the container.

Sarah's stomach churned, and wanted to empty the junk food she had fed it the night before. The palm of her hand pressed to her mouth to suppress the gagging noises she made.

The henchmen were drawing closer as she moved faster toward Rick.

"We need to find them. I'm not going back to Kinnerk without having something useful," one of the men said. "I've seen what he does when he's pissed. It's not pretty."

Rick kept his finger pressed to his lips and reached out with his free hand.

Sarah hit the end of the roll off and removed her palm. She let out a subtle breath of air.

Madness Rising

Rick pointed to a sheet of dense plastic that was draped over the side of the building. The wind caught the edges and thrashed the material.

An opening within the exterior wall caught Sarah's attention. He'd found a way inside.

"There's no use in hiding. We will find you," the lead henchman yelled down the alley. "Come out now, and we can settle our business, then you two can be on your merry little way. Scouts honor."

The snickering from the men was subtle, but still loud enough to be heard. They weren't trying to hide their devious intentions.

Neither Sarah nor Rick muttered a single syllable in response. They kept their mouths sealed and slipped between the plastic into the dark structure.

They traversed over busted brick that lay scattered over the concrete foundation. The shifting of the chunks of clay under their feet gripped them by the short hairs.

"Where the hell do we go?" Sarah asked, her voice low and filled with panic.

"No clue," Rick answered as they moved down the hallway. "We keep moving until we've lost them."

Sarah turned the way they came in. The boisterous goons shouted at one another as their silhouettes loomed beyond the veil. No doubt they'd discover the opening behind the plastic sheeting soon.

The hallway stretched for what seemed like forever. The rooms that resided on both sides of the hallway were missing doors and had just as much debris and trash within their spaces. Large sections of walls were missing, making it challenging to hide.

Both Rick and Sarah searched for a way out as they fumbled down the dim hallway. With blackness clinging to the space, they struggled to find the exit.

The henchmen approached the covering. The crunching of the plastic material ripped a sharp breath of fright from Sarah. She stopped, then spun around to the hole in the side of the building.

Rick tapped her shoulder from the flight of steps beside her. Blinding darkness cloaked his body, leaving only a vague outline for her to see. He motioned with his hand and tilted his head toward the ether.

Sarah wasn't keen on venturing up into the bowels of the crumbling building, but they didn't have a choice. They had to keep moving, and put some distance between them and their aggressors. She was hopeful that they'd find another way out of the building.

The wooden steps creaked a warning as they traversed the aged stairs.

The henchmen entered the building, loud and careless. The shifting of the clay bricks, followed by a dense thump echoed down the silent hallway. Grumbling and more shouting chased after Sarah as they hit the first landing.

Rick paused, then glanced back down to the hallway. The raised voices of the thugs carried within the framework of the structure. It was easy to track where they were, but also made it unsettling as they drew closer to their current position.

Sarah repositioned her fingers over the grip of the Glock as she gulped. Sweat populated the surface of her palm which made her hands slippery and clammy.

"We move up to the next floor, and see if we can find another way out of here," Rick whispered.

Sarah tilted her head.

Madness Rising

The outline of his arm moved behind his back. He retrieved the Glock that was secured in the waistband of his jeans. Rick chambered a round, then nodded toward the next flight of stairs.

They raced up the stairs as the henchmen loomed at the base of the staircase on the first floor. Each footfall made Sarah cringe from the slight creak in the steps.

Rick hit the landing that opened to a cavernous hallway. Small beams of light shone through the numerous holes that littered the high ceilings. Nestled between the dull rays of light, patches of darkness resided.

Mounds of busted wood and sheetrock covered the floors. The walls along the hallway had more gaping holes punched through them, and beyond that, blackness.

Rick advanced, slow and cautious, with Sarah in tow as he looked either way.

The hairs on the back of Sarah's neck stood on end. A tingling sensation slithered up her spine as the stairs creaked. She turned toward the pit of blackness with her Glock clutched with both hands.

Trepidation built inside of her. The lump, lodged in her throat, wouldn't go down, regardless of how many times she swallowed.

Sarah took a step back with the Glock trained at the staircase. "I think they're heading up this way. We need to find a place to hide now."

Rick agreed with a dip of his chin. His fingernails scratched at the scruff on the side of his face as he searched for a place for them to take cover.

Sarah covered their backs, giving Rick time to plot out their next move.

Heavy feet punished the staircase from below, followed by chatter from the henchmen.

A strident beam of bright white light tore through the darkness from the landing below, and played over the busted drywall. The chatter of the men crept up the stairs as the light grew wider.

"It's madness out there right now," a high-pitched voice said. "At least we won't have to worry too much about the police. They've got their hands full with the city burning down around them. I bet we're the least of their worries."

"Just concentrate on what we're doing here, all right," a gruff voice shot back. "I'm looking to get my cut as fast as possible, so we find these two and handle business. No messing around."

"Who? Me?" the high-pitched voice guffawed.

"Case in point. Just shut up and focus, will ya?"

"Sure thing, buzz kill."

Rick tapped her arm, then nodded to his left. He moved down the hallway at a good clip with Sarah a few paces behind.

"They're upstairs," a voice said, shouting at the top of his lungs. "Find them, now! We can't let them get away."

Sarah peered over her shoulder at the landing as light shone from the dark staircase.

Rick and Sarah skirted the blind corner of the hallway in a dead sprint. Each step sounded like thunder striking the building.

"Watch out," Rick said, as he stumbled to the side. He lost his balance and slammed into the drywall with a dense thud.

Sarah spotted the hole in the floor, but was unable to react and skirt the damaged area. Her foot punched through the rotting wood with ease. Gravity forced her frame down through the floor. The Glock fell from her hand and bounced over the wooden planks as her fingers searched for anything to grab. She found a loose plank that stopped her descent before plummeting to the dark depths below.

Rick pushed away from the wall and reached for Sarah. "Hold on. I got you."

Panic flooded Sarah. The tips of her fingers held tough as she tried to pull herself up.

Rick grabbed under her arm and pulled toward him. Sarah lifted some, but stopped. Something tugged at her and kept her from moving much farther.

The henchmen were inbound, running hard and fast in their direction. It wouldn't take them long to make the bend. Rick and Sarah needed to stop them before they made it that far.

"I got this. Just hold them off for a few minutes while I pull myself out." Sarah strained to pull herself out.

"Damn it." Rick stood up. He stepped around Sarah and ran for the edge of the hallway.

"They're down this way!" High-pitch yelled.

Gunfire sounded off, making Sarah flinch. She caught sight of the muzzle fire from Rick's Glock out of the corner of her eye. Each round fired in the corridor hammered her ears and made her squint.

The jagged pieces of wood stabbed her torso like tiny needles. Her eyes watered as she fought through the pain.

More gunfire ensued with the henchmen unloading their magazines. The cacophony of bullets sounded like angry wasps swarming the building. The busting of sheetrock and plaster melded with the violent, rhythmic beat of the standoff.

Sarah pulled harder as the sharp ends of the busted planks penetrated her chest. A welp of pain fled her mouth. More tears raced down her flushed, sweaty cheeks.

She pushed through the agony.

The tips of the wood snapped, freeing her from their hold. She continued to pull herself out of the pit that sought to swallow her.

"Come and get us, you dirty Irish bastards." Rick snarled as he popped off three more rounds.

The floor under Sarah quaked as Rick darted from the corner of the corridor. He unloaded his magazine as she pulled her legs out.

What the hell is he doing? she thought.

The skin around her chest and stomach stung. Her shirt was wet with a mixture of sweat and blood which made the fabric stick to her tacky flesh.

The pain from her chest grew, but she didn't have time to think about it. Certain death was right around the corner.

More yelling from the henchmen echoed through the deserted halls. The gunfire had ceased for the moment.

Sarah rolled to her back, panting as her heart pressed against her chest. No light was visible from the adjoining hallway. Where was Rick?

She gulped, then flipped over to her side. Her hand rubbed at the stab marks on her torso as she searched for the Glock. It was to the side of the gaping hole in the floor against the wall, out of her reach.

Shouting loomed from the adjoining hallway, followed by thunderous crashing.

Sarah scurried to her knees, then feet as she stumbled to get her piece. The planks of wood creaked, signaling her position to any threats nearby. Sarah grabbed the Glock, turned, and sagged against the wall, feeling spent and depleted of energy.

The heavy footfalls rushed her way. The cat was out of the bag. The henchmen were coming, and this time, they wouldn't be fooled.

Madness Rising

CHAPTER FOUR

SARAH

R ick was gone, but was he dead?

His fate ate at Sarah as she traversed the endless halls of the creepy building. She hadn't heard from him, or anymore gunfire for that matter. It was difficult to not assume the worst.

Instead, Sarah focused on putting as much distance between her and the men tracking her down as possible.

The henchmen were relentless—like blood hounds that caught a whiff of blood and stayed the course.

The rotting floors creaked and gave with each step Sarah took. A mixture of cavernous holes and smaller portions of missing planks made it dangerous and challenging to navigate.

It was an endless maze of corridors that zigged and zagged with large sections of walls missing. It looked as though the building was in the early stages of being renovated, or just gutted before they tore the eyesore down.

Sarah skirted another mound of busted sheetrock that had 2 X 4's protruding from the middle of the debris. The nail-infested boards looked like some sort of creature with fangs. She lost her footing and stumbled across the floor to the far wall.

The henchmen had fallen back some, giving her a bit of reprieve.

But she was lost.

Her face twisted in uncertainty as she breathed heavily. The injured areas on Sarah's torso were sore to the touch.

She looked about the defunct space, trying to determine which way she needed to go. It felt as though she was trudging through quicksand.

The handles of her purse slid down her shoulder. It didn't want to stay in place. She lifted the leather straps over her head to her other shoulder, and slid the purse toward her back.

The floor creaked down the hall in the direction she had come from. Sarah trained an attentive ear and listened past the thumping of blood that pulsated in her head.

Only one set of footsteps could be heard. It was that, or they were walking in tandem with one another, which didn't make sense. Perhaps they split up to cover more ground.

Sarah ejected the magazine to her Glock. A few rounds sat ready to do what was needed. She had another magazine in her purse at one time, but it was missing now. Maybe taken by the thug that mugged her a day or so ago.

She slapped the magazine back into place, then glanced at the 2X4s. A thought gelled in her head as the footfalls crept closer.

Sarah grabbed one of the boards, taking care to not slice her hand or forearm open on the rusty ends of the nails.

The weighted wood consumed most of her hand. It was stout and felt solid. She shuffled down the hall and slipped inside one of the drab rooms.

The darkness swallowed her as she paused in the entrance. Slivers of light bled through the narrow fissures within the wall across the space. It wasn't much, but enough to give her the lay of the land.

There was no furniture of any kind or other large objects she could take cover behind. More debris littered the floors and within the space. It wasn't ideal, but it would have to do.

The thug was close. The clomp of his feet down the hall signaled his position.

Sarah scooted down the wall and stopped shy of the gaping hole within the drywall. She set the 2X4 on the floor, and leaned it against the sheetrock—a backup weapon in case she needed it.

The Glock trembled in her grasp.

Fear racked Sarah through and through, much like how the Creeper, the man stalking her, made her feel unsafe and on edge with just a single thought.

A heavy sigh lingered from the hallway, followed by a huff of anger. Her pursuer had caught up to her, but wasn't sure where she was. She had no place left to go, and hoped he'd move on past the room she was hiding in.

Sarah held her breath. The pounding of her heart sounded like a snare drum. She feared the thug would detect the loud thumping from the hall.

"Where is this bitch at?" the thug asked in frustration.

Wood splintered and cracked from the room across from her. More sighs loomed large from the agitated man.

Sarah closed her eyes and fought to control her breathing. A spike of adrenaline surged through her as the ruckus from the other room ceased.

Madness Rising

Light shone through the hole in the wall next to Sarah. She tightened up her shoulders, and leaned to the side, away from the opening.

The enraged man stomped across the hall to the room Sarah was hiding in. The light vanished, then reappeared at the entrance to the space.

She trained the Glock at the doorway and waited for the thug to crest the jamb. Her finger rested on the trigger as the light grew brighter and larger along the far wall.

The tip of his boot stepped inside the room, followed by a tiny portion of his body. Sarah didn't have a clear shot yet. The jamb of the door protected him, whether he knew it or not.

She leaned forward and craned her neck, trying to get a better bead on her pursuer. He milled about for a few seconds as the light played over the room. The strident beam cut to the side in Sarah's direction.

In a panic, she leaned back and brushed against the wall. Her weight nudged the rotting drywall enough to make a subtle sound.

Sarah cringed.

The light froze in her direction. He had found her.

The man's arm stretched into the room with a pistol fixed in his grasp. The light lit up the tattoo on the man's forearm. It looked familiar, but she couldn't place where she had seen it before.

Sarah opened fire.

The Glock barked and recoiled in her hand.

Fire spat from the barrel.

The frame around the door splintered as the bullets tore through the rotted wood. The henchman took cover behind the wall.

Sarah emptied the magazine in a matter of seconds. She dropped the piece and reached for the 2X4.

The thug returned fire from around the corner of the jamb. Two rounds popped off in quick succession.

The bullets whizzed past her shoulder, grazing her shirt. They impacted the far wall with a dense thud.

Sarah swung the 2X4 like a Louisville Slugger. The rusted fangs of the board sunk into the man's hand, knocking the gun free of his hold.

"Awww. Christ." The pistol rattled on the floor as he jerked his injured hand back. Sarah wrenched the nails from the thugs' trembling hand as he charged into the space. "You're going to pay for that, bitch."

Sarah swung the 2X4 again with everything she had.

The board slammed into the man's side and knocked him against the wall. The flashlight fell from his grasp and clanged off the floor. His boot struck the metal casing and sent it flying across the room.

Sarah pulled the board away to dish out more punishment. He grabbed the stout piece of wood with a firm grip, then knocked it free of her hand.

The 2X4 clanged off the floor at her feet. Sarah's eyes went wide with terror as the brute gnashed his teeth.

She lunged for the board.

The thug kicked it away, well out of her reach. He loomed before Sarah. The light from the flashlight cast his shadow on the wall which made him look like a giant.

Blood dribbled from his hand and side and splattered on the floor. His fingers flexed, then balled into a fist that ripped a growl from the scowl on his face.

Sarah was trapped like a rat in a maze with a voracious cat ready to tear the tiny animal to shreds.

The hulking man narrowed his gaze. The shadow cast across his face made him look more sinister. His wide frame blocked her path to the doorway. Weaponless and with no way out, she attempted one plea for her life.

"Listen, I don't know anything about the money you're after," Sarah pleaded through shuddering lips. She held her hands up in front of her as the brute forced her into the far corner of the room. "I don't even know Allen or anything else pertaining to your boss. Please, just let me and my friend go."

The thug's scowl remained. He didn't bat an eye at her feeble attempt to save her and Rick's life.

"Bullshit," the man snarled. "Then why the hell did you nearly run us over back at his garage?" He held up his good hand before Sarah could answer. "Let me tell you why. It's because you know where that piece of trash Allen is or you're in on whatever little plan that weasel hatched. Either way, I'm going to enjoy finding out what you know." His tone shifted. The scowl on his face twisted to a demented smirk that made Sarah feel unclean. His tongue slithered from his mouth like a snake and licked around his lips.

Oh God.

Sarah wasn't going to allow what was coming next. She'd fight with everything she had until the last bit of life left her body.

She took off in a dead sprint, trying to skirt past the vile man. He snatched her up in his tree trunk like arms with minimal effort.

"No. Let me go, you bastard." Sarah screamed at the top of her lungs while kicking her legs.

The man turned with his back to the wall. His strong arms held firm, despite Sarah's thrashing.

Her legs kicked wildly, and her arms swung in every direction with the hopes of catching a lucky shot on the man's face.

She dipped her chin and searched for the 2X4.

"Let's begin, shall we?"

Sarah leaned into the man's broad chest, then tossed her head back. Her skull connected with the bridge of the thug's nose.

"Christ," he said, yelling into her ear. His grip lessened, giving Sarah a bit of wiggle room.

She threw her upper body forward and pushed her legs toward his. The tilting of her body pulled him toward the floor. Her feet hit solid ground, but his hold around her chest remained.

Sarah bent down, then drove the man back into the wall. The sheetrock caved in.

His arms dropped from around Sarah, giving her space to flee. He roared aloud as he cupped his nose.

Sarah stumbled across the floor and grabbed the 2X4. The enraged man hammered the wall with his balled fist and the tip of his boot, busting the drywall more.

She rose from the floor as he turned and looked her way. Blood seeped from both nostrils. He snarled at her.

Sarah backed away with the dense plank of wood clutched in her hands. She eyed the doorway for a split second before focusing on her aggressor.

The man took a single step forward. Two arms emerged through the hole in the wall. They wrapped around his throat and yanked him backward.

Shock flooded the man's face as he smashed through the crumbling wall. Dust tainted the air as busted pieces of sheetrock fell to the floor.

The strife from the men fighting loomed from the corridor. A loud crash made her flinch. Sarah stood in place, wielding the makeshift weapon as she craned her neck toward the battling men in the hallway.

It has to be Rick.

A gunshot rang out, followed by a flash of white.

A heavy thump hit the floor.

Madness Rising

No sounds loomed from the corridor except panted breathing.

Sarah retreated to the doorway, stumbling over her feet. She struggled to control her breathing. Short bursts escaped her mouth as she toed the sill.

Movement from the hallway controlled any hasty actions Sarah contemplated. She hoped Rick survived, but she couldn't be sure.

"Sarah," a weak voice said from the hallway. "Are you all right?"

Relief washed over Sarah. She recognized the voice. "Yeah. I'm good." She stepped out into the corridor and lowered the 2X4.

Rick was on the ground with his back against the wall. The thug's large frame was draped across his waist. His face was contorted in exhaustion. He rolled the dead man's bulk from his legs. "I'm glad you're ok."

Sarah rushed to his side while keeping a watchful eye on the thug lying prone on his stomach. "You too. I wasn't sure if they got you or not." She extended her hand out.

Rick grabbed it. "Not for lack of trying. That's for damn sure."

He groaned in discomfort as Sarah pulled him to his feet. What little she could see of his face was dirty with dark patches of black she assumed was blood.

"You're hurt."

"I'll live. Not the worst shape I've ever been in."

Sarah looked past Rick to the other end of the corridor.

"How many are left? He's the only one I've seen. Not sure where the other guy is that was with him."

"I took one out on my way here. I think it was the high-pitched dirtbag that was with our friend here, which means we have two remaining. They no doubt heard that gunshot." Rick ejected the magazine from his Glock, then grumbled in frustration. "I'm out."

"Do you think they'll come? Maybe they'll give up and cut their losses." Sarah hoped that was the case, but deep down, she didn't feel like they'd just abandon a lead, whether it was viable or not.

Rick slapped the empty mag into place, then secured the Glock in the waistband of his jeans behind his back. "Doubtful. I know of Kinnerk. He's a ruthless son of a bitch and doesn't let things slide. His goons are still here somewhere. They won't dare go back to him empty handed. Not if they value their lives."

A sinking feeling filled the pit of Sarah's stomach. The henchmen were down two men, but that did little to stay her nerves.

They were out of ammo and lost in the confines of the sprawling, abandoned building. "What are we going to do, then? I emptied my Glock at this asshole earlier."

Rick rubbed his chin, then ran his fingers through his hair. Sarah suspected he was formulating a plan to get the hell out of there. "Is there a flashlight in there?"

"Yeah, there is," Sarah answered. "I'll be right back."

She rushed into the room, searching for the thug's flashlight. It had been kicked against the wall.

Sarah retrieved the small light and her Glock, then ran back out into the hallway. "Got it."

Rick kneeled next to the dead man's body. He patted him down around his waist. "Shine the light over here, will ya?" He worked his fingers into the front pockets of the man's jeans.

As Sarah watched him search the body, she caught sight of the tattoo on the man's forearm. A portion of the design was concealed by shadows and the man's head. She cocked her head to the side, then squinted her eyes.

Madness Rising

A symbol of some sort, or so she assumed. She grabbed his hand and pulled his arm out from under his big head.

"What are you doing?" Rick asked.

Sarah skimmed over the design. A Celtic Knot that was different than the traditional symbol. It had dark, endless loops that were woven together with no beginning or ending. Additional markings were etched around the outside which were Greek to her. "I've seen this tattoo before."

Rick glanced at the man's arm. "Yeah. It's a Celtic Knot. Pretty common."

"No. It's not that," she said, muttering under her breath.

"Guess this will have to do. Better than nothing, I suppose." Rick pulled a knife from the man's pant pocket. He stood up, holding the blade in his hand.

A faint light at the far end of the corridor sliced through the dimness like a knife.

Sarah noticed the beam as she pondered on the marking she'd discovered tattooed on the man's arm.

"Hey," Rick said, waving his hand in front of Sarah's face. "Snap out of it. They're heading this way."

Sarah shook her head. "Yeah. Sorry." She glanced down the hallway in the opposite direction. "Come on. Let's get going while we can. There's got to be another way out of here somewhere."

Rick stared at the knife, then down the hall at the inbound henchmen. He jerked his head the other way. "You go. I'm going to end this here."

Confusion swirled in Sarah's mind. "Huh? What do you mean?"

"It's because of me that they're after us. If we wouldn't have stopped by Allen's garage, then this wouldn't have happened," Rick said. "If I handle it here, then we should be in the clear. No one else knows what we look like or our names. You won't have to worry about this anymore. Now, go. I'll catch up to you."

The tromping of the incoming goons grew louder as did the light at the other end of the hall. If Sarah was going to make it down the hallway before they made the bend, she had to leave now.

Racked with indecision, Sarah back-peddled away as Rick stayed behind. "242 Ricketts St. Cascade Villas. Apartment ten B."

Rick wrenched his chin toward the opposite end of the hall, away from the incoming footfalls. "Got it, now go."

Madness Rising

CHAPTER FIVE

RUSSELL

Russell was a magnet for trouble, and the law. He knew the dance all too well.

His string of bad luck showed no signs of slowing down or stopping. Not only had he managed to get himself arrested, but Cathy was kidnapped, Thomas hurt, and he was that much further away from getting to Sarah.

Crammed in the backseat of the sheriff's cruiser, he peered through the window with a defeated gaze. His shoulders sagged as his head drooped forward.

The sheriff peered at Russell through the rearview mirror. His beady eyes stuck to Russell like glue. Russell could feel judgement from the portly sheriff, but he didn't care. Innocent or guilty, he had to find a way out of the pickle he was in.

Madness Rising

"You're not from around here, are you?" the sheriff asked as he hooked a left through the non-working intersection. "I can't say that I've seen you around town before."

"Nope. Just passing through is all," Russell replied. "Where did they take the dogs?"

Thomas was taken to the town's local hospital to get checked out further before the sheriff would question him.

"The shelter, for now, until we can get to the bottom of things. They'll be properly taken care of there."

The handcuffs around Russell's wrists were tight. The metal ends bit into the bone. It was uncomfortable, but bearable. He didn't want to complain. The last thing he wanted to do was grind on the sheriff's nerves. At least, not about anything as insignificant as a little discomfort.

"What's going to happen with Cathy?" Russell asked. "The longer you wait to act, the better the chance something bad will happen to her. I've seen a ton of crap happen over the past few days. Her life is in danger. Believe me."

The sheriff hooked a right, drove a bit more, then swung into an empty parking spot in front of the station. "We'll look into it as fast as we can, but our plates are overflowing with problems. Not sure if you've noticed the whole power issue or not. It's kind of a big deal at the moment." His sardonic tone wasn't lost on Russell, or subtle for that matter.

Russell rolled his eyes, then glanced out of the window.

A single Prowler was parked next to them. He glanced to the sheriff's station and squinted his eyes. Russell couldn't spot any movement through the glass doors of the dark building. He was curious to the size of the police force since he knew nothing about Luray.

The sheriff killed the engine, then threw open his door. He wormed his way out of the driver's seat, then hopped down to the pavement. He opened Russell's door and motioned for him to get out.

Russell slid out, and took a step back, allowing the sheriff to close the door.

The town was silent, still even. There weren't many, if any people milling about the shops and other businesses. In the distance, Russell could hear the faint whisper of sirens calling.

"Quaint town you have here, Sheriff," Russell said. "Doesn't seem to be much traffic."

The sheriff grabbed the back of Russell's arm and pulled. "With the power being out pretty much everywhere, most folks have stayed at home. Nothing else to do. We've had our hands full, though, with patrolling 24/7, and responding to fires. We've had a handful of older buildings in town catch fire from sparking transformers that blew, along with some just outside the city. We're not sure what's caused the transformers to blow and catch fire, but we're keeping an eye on things as best we can."

Russell wondered how close of an eye they were really keeping. The sheriff seemed less than concerned with what he had been told. Procedure or not, Russell figured he'd at least show a bit more urgency. Maybe Cathy was right about the portly cop. Maybe he was dirty.

The sheriff opened the door and escorted Russell inside. They passed through another set of double glass doors that led into the main entrance of the station.

The open blinds allowed natural light to fill the space. Small tabletop lanterns were positioned on top of the desks around the large office. There weren't any officers around. The station looked abandoned.

"Running on a skeleton crew, huh?" Russell asked.

Madness Rising

"We're managing along as best we can under the circumstances. Trying to keep the peace and the riff raff from tearing anything up. I'd be out there right now, but someone was discharging a firearm in the middle of town like a war zone."

A pop shot at Russell. He didn't bite. He kept his attention straight ahead and his mouth shut as the sheriff escorted him to an empty chair next to a cluttered desk.

Russell sat down, then peered over the lull that consumed the station.

The sheriff pulled out his rolling chair from his desk and plopped down. "All right, son, let's get the basics out of the way before we get down to business here. What's your full name?"

"Russell Cage."

"Where do you reside?"

"Boston."

"You got any family there?"

Russell sighed, then hesitated. "Yes. My wife, Sarah."

The sheriff cut his eyes to Russell, letting him know that he heard him. He shook his head, then continued. "How do you know Cathy Snider and Thomas Kinkade?"

"They helped me out of a tight jam a few days ago," Russell answered.

"What sort of jam?" the sheriff asked.

Russell dipped his chin and thought of Tim, his best friend who perished in the plane crash they were in a few days ago.

"Me and my friend, Tim, were in a plane that went down in the mountains. Lost power or engine problems. I don't know. He didn't survive the crash. I barely got out before the plane dumped over the side of a cliff."

The sheriff nodded while looking at Russell with a peculiar stare. "Pretty lucky that you survived and he didn't, wouldn't you say?"

Russell didn't care for what the portly man was insinuating.

His brow furrowed and lips grew taut. "I guess, but in the end, my best friend died in that plane. I would have died out there or been eaten by a damn mountain lion if it wasn't for Cathy and Max."

He didn't have time for such meaningless procedures that weren't accomplishing anything. "Listen, Sheriff, those two guys back there hit us on purpose, then kidnapped Cathy. They work for Marcus Wright. His men have been terrorizing Cathy and Thomas for the past few days and beyond that as far as I know. They've almost succeeded in killing us a handful times. They burned down Cathy's cabin and stormed Thomas's house."

The sheriff set his pen down, then leaned back in his chair. He rubbed his second chin, then said, "Those are some serious accusations to be making. Especially for one of Luray's most influential residents."

"Cathy mentioned that she had put in some complaints with you about his men trespassing and harassing her. It's not hard here to connect the dots," Russell said.

"She did put in some complaints, and we have spoken with Mr. Wright. He has apologized for any misunderstandings. We're keeping a close eye on things, though." The sheriff rapped his fingers against the files stacked on his desk. "As far as the fire at her place, and what transpired at Mr. Kinkade's place, we'll look into everything and see what we come up with. Things aren't happening too quickly, but it will be looked into at some point."

Russell felt as though the sheriff was putting him off. "If it'll help any, I caught the first three digits of the truck's license plate, which is a black Ford extended cab truck."

42

Madness Rising

The sheriff grabbed his pen, then said, "Anything will be helpful. We won't be able to search through any databases with the power out, but we can keep an eye out for the vehicle. We'll also check with Mr. Wright as well."

"VBK is all I got off the plate," Russell replied. "The truck was speeding away and swerving, so I couldn't get the rest before it got too far away."

"It's not much, but we'll see," the sheriff said. He paused, then said, "Do you drink much, Mr. Cage?"

The question caught Russell off guard. He shifted in the uncomfortable chair as he cleared his throat. "I do on occasion, much like most folks I'd imagine. Is that a crime in Luray, Sheriff?"

"No, not at all," the sheriff replied. "When's the last time you had a taste?"

"Last night," Russell said, tersely. He had nothing to hide. He wasn't drunk, at the moment, anyway. The line of questioning, though, grated on his nerves. His voice raised an octave as he expressed his frustration. "I'm not sure what any of this has to do with what has happened and finding Cathy."

The sheriff's hand motioned as if it was going down to his sidearm. "I'll tell you what it has to do with, Mr. Cage. I've got a suspect, who has been drinking, was in an accident, and discharging a weapon in town recklessly. That's a trifecta of bad shit."

Russell could see where this was going. "So, you're going to book me, then? Is that what you're getting at here?"

The rustling of keys caught Russell's attention from behind. Static hissed from the two-way radio sitting on the sheriff's desk. He snatched the radio and listened closely.

It was hard to make out from the white noise. A distorted voice muttered from the speaker.

"This is Sheriff Donner, say your last, over." The sheriff held the radio closer to his ear and removed his thumb.

Russell couldn't make out what was being said. It all sounded like a garbled mess from where he was sitting.

Sheriff Donner nodded, then looked up from his desk. He lifted his free arm in the air and waved his hand.

The squeaking of shoes over the tile floor played in Russell's ear. He glanced over his shoulder at the officer weaving through the maze of empty desks.

"Yeah. I'll head over there right now," the sheriff said.

The slender officer flanked Russell with his hands resting on his duty belt. "We got another issue, Sheriff?" The deputy's voice was young with a slight country twang to it. His hair was slicked back over his head as he chewed on what Russell assumed was gum.

Sheriff Donner grumbled as he set the radio down on his desk. A sigh fled his plump lips as his hand rubbed up and down his face. "More of the same, Johnson. We have some folks over at the supermarket trying to steal food. It's put everyone over there on edge. A fight broke out, and well, shit rolled down hill. I tell you what, the longer this blackout goes on, the worse it's going to get around here, I'm afraid."

"Do you know, by chance, how wide spread it is?" Russell asked.

Sheriff Donner stood from his chair and pushed it away. "We heard most of the eastern side of the country, but that can't be confirmed. Only thing working at the moment are two-way radios and HAMS."

Deputy Johnson nodded toward the main entrance, then said, "You want me to handle this one? You've been going nonstop since the power went out. I haven't seen you sleep or eat much the last few days."

Madness Rising

"No. I got it," Sheriff Donner said, with a subtle shake of his head and a flick of his wrist. "I've got a few other stops I need to make afterward. Check in on some of our older folks. Make sure they're doing all right."

"Copy that," Deputy Johnson replied. "What are we doing with him?"

Sheriff Donner looked at Russell, who was still seated next to his desk. "Put him in one of the interrogation rooms for right now until I get back, and we can continue our conversation."

"And how long is that going to be?" Russell scoffed. "Cathy needs you now, not later. Can you not call in someone else? I mean, you have your deputy here."

"It'll take however long is needed," Sheriff Donner said, in a curt, cold manner. He leaned on the edge of the desk and narrowed his beady eyes at Russell. "I suggest you worry about yourself, son. The more you run your mouth, the deeper the shit gathers around your legs. If you want to get back to that wife of yours in Boston anytime soon, I'd suggest you zip it."

Deputy Johnson grabbed Russell by the arm and yanked him out of the chair. "Come on, tough guy."

Russell looked at the sheriff, but didn't venture a counter remark. The blow hard was right about one thing, he was sinking further into a messed-up situation that wasn't getting better.

"Keep an eye on him," Sheriff Donner said, while grabbing his two-way from the desk. "If you need anything, get me on the radio."

"I got this. He won't be any trouble."

Sheriff Donner strode past Russell and made for the main entrance. He clipped the radio on his hip, and threw the doors open to the station.

Deputy Johnson grabbed Russell by the wrist and the scruff of his flannel shirt. He led him through the dimness of the station toward a dark hallway.

"You know, your sheriff is making a mistake here. Those men who took Cathy are dangerous. Who knows what they have planned for her?" Russell pleaded his case.

He was escorted down the hall which grew darker from the lack of windows in that section of the station.

"Are you referring to Cathy Snider?" Deputy Johnson asked.

"Yeah, I am," Russell answered as he turned to the side to look at the officer. Deputy Johnson jerked him about face. Russell stumbled. "Listen. I'm telling the truth here. I know for a fact that Marcus Wright has taken her. The man is dangerous."

Deputy Johnson jerked Russell's shirt, stopping him in his tracks in front of a dark blue door with a small window embedded within its core. Russell couldn't read what was inscribed on the plate just below the glass, but figured it was the interrogation room.

"Are you some sort of family friend or boy toy hanging around her place?"

Russell sighed, and shook his head. "Family friend, I guess. I don't know. She helped me out."

Deputy Johnson shoved him forward into the door.

The side of Russell's faced slammed against the cold, hard steel. The impact caught him off guard. A twinge of pain stabbed his skull as he shook his head.

"Don't turn around or move again until I tell you to."

"What the hell," Russell said, protesting the deputy's less than gentle touch. "You know, I do have rights here."

Deputy Johnson jerked Russell back from the door, then leaned in close to whisper in his ear. "Your rights are whatever I deem them to be and every word that tumbles out of your mouth gets you one step closer to drowning. Besides, I wouldn't worry about Mrs. Snider. She's in good hands."

Russell's eyes bulged.

It seemed that corruption had infested the Luray Sheriff's Department and taken root.

Derek Shupert

CHAPTER SIX

SARAH

Brave but stupid was a perfect way to describe Rick. He shouldered the brunt of responsibility for dragging her into the muddled mess that was Kinnerk's goons, even if it was by accident.

She didn't feel as though it warranted him staying behind to deal with the remaining thugs, but he was determined to make things right. They had the upper hand, and could've gained some distance between their pursuers, but in the end, guilt, like most things, could weigh a person down to the point where they'd do whatever they felt was right to set things straight.

Raised voices and shouting trailed Sarah and faded away as she navigated the hallways of the abandoned building. She kept moving, searching for a way out of the defunct space.

Everything looked the same within the murk that clung to every square inch of the condemned building. It was an endless maze with no way out.

The faint report of gunfire stopped her cold. Dread and sadness washed over her as she checked behind her. The flashlight's strident beam of light trained at the stretch of dim corridor before her.

No shadowy figures loomed in the distance or beams of light that indicated a threat, or Rick, was inbound.

A sheen of wetness coated each eye. Her hand trembled as she listened for any inbound footfalls rushing her way. None could be heard. Even the raised voices had been squashed.

Rick. You damn fool.

She hoped he wasn't on the receiving end of the discharging weapon, but the silence did little to ease her worry.

Sarah waited a moment longer, listening and watching the dimness before she got back on the move. A sliver of hope beckoned her to wait, or even go back to see if he was all right. Afterall, he had gone out of his way for a stranger he barely knew.

The fear was too great, though, and so was the drive to get to her best friend. Both drove her legs onward, whether Sarah wanted it to or not.

The light in her hand guided her through the bowels of the structure. Large sections of the floor were either missing or rotted away to the point where it looked unstable to pass. The last thing Sarah needed was to fall through the floor and break her legs. She wasn't keen to have the building as her final resting place.

Sarah ducked into the unsettling rooms nearby and slipped through gaping holes within the walls. They dumped her out into a familiar hallway.

Madness Rising

The vaulted ceiling above jogged her memory. She shined the light up toward the cracked and crumbling drywall as she took a single step forward.

The soles of her shoes rolled over something round and dense. Sarah paused, then stepped back. She tilted the beam down toward the dusty, wooden floor and found shell casings.

Dark, red spots speckled the floor around the brass casings and trailed off down the hallway.

Sarah checked behind her, ensuring she wasn't being flanked. She turned about face and shone the light at the floor a few paces ahead of her.

There was blood on the floor, but whose was it?

The red drops were covered in dust and had been trampled. More shell casings were scattered about, but no bodies could be seen.

The fear of the men looking for Sarah pushed her to escape the building before they managed to track her down.

She swept both sides of the hallway. The light didn't reveal any threats lurking within the confines of the rooms around her. She spotted an open space that had what appeared to be stairs descending down.

Finally.

The staircase they used when heading up to the first floor was dead ahead. Although relieved, Sarah approached the dark opening with caution. More of Kinnerk's men could have shown up, or some other low-life for that matter. She didn't know, and that troubled her some.

She craned her neck, and hit the landing of the rickety staircase. With her back to the wall, she peered out from the bend and scouted out the area.

The light washed over the fissures within the walls and worn, tattered planks of wood. No threats were seen or heard which relieved Sarah.

Kinnerk's men were like bulls in a china shop and didn't believe in stealth. They were loud and gave their position away most times without thought. That was the only saving grace that Sarah liked about the vile henchmen. Their confidence was their ultimate downfall.

Sarah stepped away from the cover of the wall and made her way down the stairs. The boards creaked under her weight. She knew it was coming. Still, the sharp warning kept her on guard, and her ears trained for any subtle footfalls from the first floor, or from the way she'd come.

So far, so good.

She was in the clear as she hit the landing and continued on to the last flight of stairs. She wanted to grab the Glock, but it would've been useless at the moment. It was nothing more than a paperweight. If push came to shove, she could hurl it or pistol whip any threats that crossed her path.

Sarah hit the last step and paused. She stayed close to the wall and checked the hallway on the first floor for any movement. Both stretches were void of any activity. The only sound she heard was that of the wind tormenting the plastic covering the hole in the side of the building.

Freedom from the structure was within Sarah's reach. Although relieved to be out of the horrid place, she couldn't help but think of Rick, and whether or not he was still alive.

It ate at her thoughts like a parasite as she bolted for the hole in the wall in a dead sprint. The side of Sarah's purse slapped her hip with each step she took. Her stride was brisk and long. She glanced to either side of the corridor, quickly checking the rooms and spaces for any potential threats waiting for her.

Madness Rising

The soles of her shoes struggled to find traction over the busted brick that laid before her. The chunks of clay shifted and moved as she sprinted out into the alleyway. Her arm swung at the plastic, knocking it out of her way as she lost her balance.

Water splashed as Sarah clomped through the small puddles. She caught herself before falling to the concrete. She took a moment to collect herself, then glanced up the side of the building.

Deep down, Sarah had faith that Rick would be all right as she had with Mandy and Russell. They had to be. With everything that had happened and was continuing to come at her, faith and hope were the only two things she had left to hold on to.

Sarah thumbed the switch to the flashlight and stowed it away in the back pocket of her trousers. She turned toward the street and jogged down the alley.

She was cautious and on edge, suspicious of any subtle sound that set off her internal alarm as she neared the sidewalk.

She stopped shy of running out into the open, and toed the corner of the building next to her. More of Kinnerk's men could be out on the streets, waiting for her or Rick to emerge. It was a notion that kept her wits sharpened and guard up. Not knowing was the hardest part.

Sarah waited for a few moments and skimmed over the immediate area for any curious gazes. The few people who passed by along the sidewalk and across the street kept their heads down, but with the chaos, and rising madness within the city, it was difficult to discern who was a threat and who wasn't.

Growling bellowed from Sarah's stomach as she wiped her palm across her sweaty brow. The stab wounds in her torso from the busted ends of the boards ached and throbbed. Her mouth felt arid, as if it were stuffed with cotton.

Water and food popped into Sarah's head, but that wasn't going to happen anytime soon. She'd have to stop eventually to regain her strength, but that time had not yet arrived. Her main priority was getting to Mandy's place. Enough time had been wasted, and she didn't want to waste anymore.

Sarah shoved her body's cravings to the side, and stepped out onto the sidewalk. Her tongue danced over her dry lips as she kept her head down. She walked at a brisk pace toward the next intersection as she skimmed over the street and nearby buildings.

For the moment, there wasn't much activity on the block. No buildings were on fire, and no people were looting businesses. Compared to what Sarah had witnessed in other parts of the city, things were relatively calm.

Sirens plagued the hazy skyline as a chopper buzzed overhead. Sarah's gaze flitted to the gray murk as a military helicopter passed overhead. It was flying low, skimming over the tops of the buildings as if searching for a place to land. The rotors of the beast drowned out any other sounds.

The tactical helicopter moved out over the road and held its position. The side of the bird facing Sarah was exposed. Uniformed men emerged from the hold and glanced down to the streets as the chopper hovered in the air.

Sarah wondered if the military was moving in to provide aid. Perhaps the National Guard had been deployed to help regain control of the populous, and bring order to the lawless land.

She stood on the tips of her toes and craned her neck, trying to see if any military ground forces were moving in from up the street. From her current position, it was difficult to see.

The chopper flew at an angle, then vanished over the buildings. The bleating of the rotors faded to a dull thumping noise that battered the air.

Madness Rising

Sarah checked behind her and searched the road. A man stood across the street, nestled behind the corner of a shop. The man retreated back within the confines of the passageway as she gazed his way.

An eerie feeling washed over Sarah as his head emerged from the alleyway once more. The bill of his hat was pulled down, concealing a portion of his face. He stared in her direction.

She looked to either side of where she was standing to see if there was anyone else nearby. For the moment, Sarah was alone.

The man emerged from the building and stood on the sidewalk. His head was tilted forward. The Boston Red Sox's symbol etched on his hat filled her gaze. He didn't move out of her way, yell at her, or excuse himself like a normal person would.

Sarah gulped, then backed away, retreating down the sidewalk.

The man lifted his head, revealing enough of his face for Sarah to see who he was.

A wiry grin slid across his face.

The life drained from Sarah in a blink. She turned white as a sheet.

The Creeper.

Derek Shupert

CHAPTER SEVEN

RUSSELL

*S*on of a bitch.

Deputy Johnson was part of Marcus's crew. His vague admission at knowing what was happening with Cathy made Russell's stomach sink. If the authorities were in bed with Marcus, then getting out of his current predicament was going to be a stretch.

Both he and Thomas could be expendable targets—loose ends that needed to be wrapped up and taken care of. A slug to the head and an unmarked grave in the vast wilderness or some sort of prison sentence that made sure he'd never see the light of day could quickly follow. Afterall, they knew where he was from now, and his wife's name.

Given the current state of things, snuffing Russell and Thomas would be easy. Calling for help would be a stretch since communications were down. He and Thomas were cut off and at the mercy of the deputy and more than likely, his sheriff.

Russell had to think on his feet and fast. There wasn't time to plot out or strategize his next move. Lives were at stake.

"You know you're not going to get away with this, right?" Russell said. "Out of you and Sheriff Donner, who do you think is the low man on the totem pole when this whole scheme crumbles down around you? I'll give you a hint. That would be you, asshole."

Deputy Johnson shoved Russell into the door again. His forearm pressed against the back of Russell's neck as he punched him in the kidneys.

The sharp strike ripped a grunt of pain from Russell's smooshed face. He gritted his teeth and blinked, clearing the wetness from his eyes. "When you two asshats get caught, and you will, do you think the sheriff is going to go down for being corrupt? He'll hang you out to dry the first chance he gets. Pin it on you. Face it. You're the scape goat."

"Whatever," Johnson growled. "You don't know dick about anything, and you're just running your mouth to save your own ass."

More pressure was applied to Russell's neck as the deputy breathed heavily in his ear.

The tips of Russell's fingers quested for the keys that dangled from the deputy's duty belt. He could hear them rattling with each hard breath that blasted his face.

"Whatever, don't believe me," Russell said, as the deputy grew angrier with each passing second, "but when the shit hits the fan, you'll hear my voice in the back of your head saying I told you so."

"You're full of-" Johnson paused, and eased up on Russell's neck. "Nice try, but it's—"

Russell pushed off the door and slammed into Deputy Johnson. He drove him back into the wall.

Madness Rising

The deputy hit the cinderblock wall and gasped. Russell spun around and kneed the corrupt cop in the midsection.

The deputy doubled over and crumbled to the tile floor as he reached for his sidearm.

"I don't think so," Russell said, as he kicked the deputy in the stomach.

Johnson coughed and hacked as he struggled to breathe. He wheezed and gasped as Russell turned and lowered to the floor. He scoured over the deputy's duty belt for the keys until they were found.

Russell unclipped the keys from Johnson's belt loop. He stood back up, and kicked Johnson again as he tried to get off the floor. "That's for punching me in the kidneys."

Johnson groaned from the floor as Russell tried each one of the keys in the lock of the cuffs.

"You're a dead man–Cage," Johnson said, breathlessly. "Not only am I going to kill–you, but that wife of yours is as good as dead as well."

Russell tuned the mouthy cop out as he focused on getting out of the cuffs. Three keys were a no go, but the fourth freed him from the shackles.

The steel cuffs unlatched from around his wrists and dropped to the floor. The indents left in his skin stung. The bone ached and hurt just by touching it.

"You're not going to do-"

Johnson swept Russell's legs, knocking him off balance. He scrambled from the floor as Russell caught himself on the wall before falling.

"Screw this. I'm just going to kill you now," Johnson said.

Russell rushed Johnson as he pulled his sidearm from its holster. Russell kept low and speared Johnson in the stomach as he fired off a single round.

The bullet grazed Russell's arm and pinged off the tile floor. It caught most of his shirt and a scant inch of flesh. A loud ring festered in his ear.

Johnson drove his elbow into Russell's spine. Each blow loosened his grip from around the deputy's waist as they charged out into the bullpen of the station.

Russell let go, then shoved Johnson backward. The deputy tumbled over a desk, knocking off the monitor and stacks of files. He hit the floor with a dense thud as Russell skirted the now crooked desk.

Johnson lifted the pistol from on his hands and knees, his finger on the trigger.

"I don't think so." Russell mashed Johnson's hand to the ground.

Another round discharged.

White flashed from the barrel as Russell pried the piece from the deputy's hand. He removed his boot from Johnson's arm and took a step back.

"Oh man. You have seriously messed up. You know that, right?" Johnson asked.

Russell trained the pistol at Johnson as he slowly stood up. "I think you're in no position to be threatening anyone."

Johnson grimaced as he used the desk as a crutch. Subtle grunts escaped through pursed lips as he glared at Russell. "What's your plan here? Kill me and flee? I can tell you right now that won't get you too far."

Russell took a step forward and grabbed a handful of Johnson's uniform. The barrel of his pistol pressed to the soft spot under his chin. "How about I just pull the trigger and we find out how far I get while they mop the bone and brain matter from the floor."

Johnson gulped as his eyes widened. "You kill me and you won't find Cathy. I can guarantee you that."

"You know where she is, then?" Russell asked.

"Maybe."

Russell shoved the barrel further into the crooked cop's skin. "It's a yes or no question, unless you want me to pull the trigger."

"No, no, no, wait," Johnson plead for his life. "I might know where they took her, but I'm not one hundred percent sure."

"What does that mean?" Russell asked.

"They never told me where they were taking her exactly," Johnson replied with a raised voice thick with fear. "He has a few places she could be at, but there's one that is kind of far outside of town. Away from any curious eyes. Lower the gun, and I'll tell you where it's at." The deputy gulped. His life hung in the balance, and he could see that Russell wasn't messing around.

"Tell me where it's at?" Russell parroted.

"Yeah, I don't think so. Do I look stupid to you?"

Russell positioned his hand over the grip.

"I'm shooting you straight here." Johnson's voice trembled and cracked as it raised an octave.

"As soon as I hit that door, you're going to double cross me, and I can't have that."

"I won't." Johnson stuttered. "You've got my word."

The deputy's word meant less than nothing. When one was faced with their own mortality, one would say and do whatever was needed to save one's hide.

No. Russell had a better idea. He had to keep an eye on Johnson, and he couldn't do that if he ventured out on his own. The moment he left the station, Johnson would set into motion a world of pain that would rain down on him. He couldn't risk Sarah's life like that, or the others for that matter.

"This is what we're going to do," Russell said. "You're going to take me to this place. I'm not letting you out of my sight."

Johnson shook his head emphatically. It was obvious he wanted no part of it, but he didn't have a choice in the matter. "No way. If he or any of his men catches me skulking around his place with you, I'm a dead man."

"Fine. Then I'll just take the info now and kill you," Russell said. "How about that?"

"How do I know you're not going to kill me either way?" he asked.

"You don't, but if you want me to decide right now, I will."

"All right." Johnson motioned with his hands for Russell to cool down and hold on. "Fine. Christ!"

Russell lowered the gun from under Johnson's chin. He took a step back, giving them a sliver of breathing room. The barrel trained at Johnson's torso as he adjusted his uniform.

"One more thing."

Johnson smoothed his shirt out as best he could, then asked, "Yeah. What's that?"

Russell backhanded Johnson. The deputy's head snapped to the side. His hands pressed to the top of the desk as blood dripped from the corner of his mouth.

"You ever threaten my wife again, and I'll kill you in the worst way possible."

Madness Rising

CHAPTER EIGHT

RUSSELL

Deputy Johnson didn't conceal his disdain for Russell. It was plastered on his face. The furrowed brow and narrowed eyes more than conveyed how he felt.

Russell couldn't have cared less. The vile man was a disgrace to the badge he wore—a piece of trash he wanted nothing more than to dispose of, but couldn't. Johnson was still an officer of the law and for now, that was the main thing keeping him alive.

"Is that your Prowler out front?" Russell asked while nodding toward the front entrance of the station.

"Yeah. It's mine," Johnson replied with a scowl.

"Good. We're taking it."

"Won't that be a bit conspicuous?" Johnson asked with a raised brow.

Madness Rising

"You work for Marcus Wright. It shouldn't surprise him if you show up," Russell answered matter-of-factly. "To be honest, I don't give a crap if he does care. You'll figure it out either way."

Johnson shook his head and snickered under his breath. He wiped the thin stream of blood from the corner of his mouth with the back of his hand. "You have no idea who you're messing with. Marcus Wright is someone you do not want to cross."

"And neither do you," Russell shot back. "Now move!" He grabbed Johnson by his uniform and shoved him toward the entrance of the station. The deputy stumbled into the doors and stopped himself before smacking into tempered glass.

On his hip, Russell spotted another pair of cuffs secured on his duty belt. He contemplated having him put them on, but he wanted him to drive, and figured that having his wrists restrained might pose more of a risk to Russell.

Johnson threw open the door in a huff and stomped through the entryway.

Russell kept a close eye on him as he pressed the barrel into the small of his back. "Just remember, you try anything other than what I tell you, I'm going to empty this magazine. You got me?"

"Yeah, I got you." Johnson shoved the next set of glass doors open as Russell escorted him out onto the sidewalk. They strode to the Prowler, calm and collected.

Russell skimmed over the buildings for any prying eyes. The town was mostly deserted. Not a single soul was visible.

Johnson tossed the driver's side door open and settled into the plush seat. He fired up the engine.

There were no other cops in the area that Russell could spot. For now, they were in the clear, and could slip away undetected. At least, until more arrived back at the station to find the disheveled mess from their scrap.

Derek Shupert

Russell opened his door and slipped into the passenger seat. He slammed it shut, then pointed the pistol toward the deputy. Johnson looked at him from the corner of his eye as he secured his seat belt.

"Come on. Let's go."

Johnson bit his tongue and did as directed. No back talk or snide remarks were offered.

Good man.

He grabbed the gear shift and pulled it into reverse. The Prowler backed away from the curb out into the street.

Russell checked the side view mirror as they headed down the road. Two animals darted around the corner of the building from the intersection flanking them. He squinted and leaned forward, watching the dogs race after them. It took a moment for Russell to figure out it was Butch and Max.

I'll be damned.

"What's wrong?" Johnson asked.

"Stop the car, and give me the keys," Russell said, turning and looking through the rear window.

"Why?" Johnson asked, confused by the request.

Russell jabbed the pistol into his side. "Because I said so, that's why."

"All right." Johnson stopped the Prowler in the middle of the street, then killed the engine. "Here."

Russell took the keys, then opened his door.

"Come on, guys," he said, patting his leg and whistling.

Both Max and Butch flanked the Prowler. Side by side, the large canines galloped toward Russell as he took a knee.

"Hey, guys. Where the heck did you come from?"

The tired dogs panted with their tongues dangling from their maws. He rubbed the crown of their heads as their tongues flicked at his face.

66

Madness Rising

Russell stood up and opened the backseat door. Both Max and Butch hopped in without being told.

"Whoa," Johnson said, twisting in his seat. "We are not taking those dogs anywhere with us."

The bulletproof glass and steel mesh cage behind the front seats kept the large, intimidating canines at bay as Johnson pointed at them.

Russell hopped back into the front seat and slammed his door.

Max bared his teeth and folded his ears as he stared at the deputy. His tongue flicked out at the frightened man.

Johnson looked to Russell with a concerned gaze.

"You're fine. Besides, this should give you ample incentive to not do anything stupid." Russell glanced back to the angry dogs as their intense, focused gazes honed in on Johnson. "They look kind of hungry, actually. Not sure when they've eaten last."

Russell relished in the deputy's quaking fear. It wasn't hard to tell from his hard gulps and wide eyes.

"Just keep them away from me, will ya?" he asked.

"Not a fan of dogs, huh?" Russell tapped the barricade with his knuckles.

Butch peered at him with his slanted, menacing eyes and licked at the glass.

"I've had some run-ins with both of them before," Johnson answered. He took the keys back and fired up the engine. He put the Prowler into drive. "Both of those mutts attacked me for no damn reason."

Russell could believe it with Butch. He was a wild card—a dog that could be triggered without much warning. He was suspect of anyone and everyone it seemed. "Perhaps they just sensed how big of a dirtbag you really are. Dogs are good at judging a person's character like that. Looks like they hit the nail on the head with you."

"Screw you, Cage," Johnson said, not caring for the slanderous remark.

"Like I said, you don't do anything stupid, and I'll make sure they leave you alone."

That was a lie and one that he couldn't guarantee he could keep. Maybe Max would listen, as it seemed like they had a pretty good rapport, but Butch was a different story all together.

From what he could tell of the hulking brute, Butch was headstrong and kind of did as he pleased. The only way Russell could even think of keeping him in line was to assert his dominance when it called for it. Show the animal who the alpha male was.

Russell kept the pistol trained at Johnson as they made their way through the desolate town. Only a handful of people were walking down the sidewalks in front of the powerless buildings. They shot a glance at the passing Prowler with a mischievous gaze that hinted at dubious intentions. Russell didn't care, much less bat an eye. Whatever they were contemplating wasn't his problem.

Silence befell the cab. No idle banter or harsh words were spoken between the two men which was fine with Russell. He didn't have much to say to the corrupt cop anyway. They had a mutual understanding of the way things were and the conditions of their arrangement.

Watching the buildings zip past, Russell couldn't help but think of Sarah and how she was doing. Being cut off from her, as he was, and not knowing how she was doing ate at him. He wished he could call her, reach out in whatever way possible just to hear her voice to make sure she was all right. That wasn't going to happen, though.

The world had plunged into dark times in a blink and the one person he wanted to be with wasn't there. Their relationship was strained because of him, and the bottles of liquor he chased to drown his own shortcomings.

Their once happy marriage was strained to the point of breaking, but there was still hope on the horizon. Despite how thin it may be, Russell had to hold onto that sliver to keep him going. To get him home for his second chance at a happy life.

They hit the outskirts of town and drove along the winding roads that sliced through the lush, mountainous hillsides. Dense wooded areas lined the narrow road and blotted out the sun overhead.

Russell peered at Johnson who had his chin dipped as he stared at Russell. "What are you looking at?"

Johnson shrugged, then shot him a quick glance before moving his attention to the road ahead of them. "When's the last time you had a fix?"

"Excuse me?" Russell asked. "Fix?"

"Your hand. The way it's shaking. I've seen that in junkies going through withdrawals," Johnson replied, nodding at Russell's trembling hand. "Drugs? Alcohol?"

Russell dipped his chin and looked at his hand. It quaked on its own, trembling on his thigh—a tick he had when his body lacked the effects of the demon's juice. One he hadn't realized was happening at that moment.

He stretched his fingers, then made a fist. "Why don't you worry about yourself and less about me?"

The last thing Russell wanted to do was talk with the corrupt deputy about anything other than what they had set out to do. He had no intentions of doing a deep dive into his shortcomings.

"I'm just saying, that's going to get a lot worse before it gets better," Johnson said, as he tilted his head at Russell's hand. "I've seen it a lot. You'll have a hard time focusing, plus hearing and seeing things that aren't there. A sort of decline into madness, really, that's hard to pull yourself out of. That descent is hard for most. Detoxing is a bitch in a controlled environment with help, but on your own, phew, you're in for a rude awakening, pal."

Russell shook his hand and furrowed his brow. "Listen, I thought I told you to-"

Johnson jerked the steering wheel clockwise. The tires of the Prowler screeched as the bulky SUV darted toward the lush verdure running along the side of the road.

Russell dumped over onto his side as the deputy grabbed the barrel of the pistol. Both Max and Butch barked and clawed at the plexiglass as the two men fought for control of the weapon.

Fire spat from the sidearm. The sharp report pounded through the enclosed space. The single round punched through the driver's side windshield at an angle as they tussled for control.

Johnson twisted the piece in Russell's hand, mashing his fingers.

"Ahh," Russell said, in pain as his contorted digit bent within the trigger guard.

The Prowler barreled through the tall weeds that lined the roadway.

Russell punched Johnson in the face. The deputy's head snapped to the side, his hand releasing its hold of the pistol.

Russell lost his grip of the pistol.

It tumbled off the center console and fell to the floorboard on Russell's side.

The Prowler flew across the road on a dime, and headed for the opposite side of the road.

Russell was thrown against the door and unable to retrieve the sidearm before the Prowler plowed through the weeds.

The front end tore through the dense vegetation at full speed and down the steep side of the hill.

Madness Rising

Johnson wrenched the steering wheel from side to side, avoiding the trees that littered the hillside. He slammed the brakes with both feet, trying to bring the two-ton steel vehicle under submission.

The wheels locked up, but the SUV kept going. Russell bent over and reached for the floorboard. The seat belt snapped to and restricted his movement. He couldn't lay eyes on the pistol from where he was. His feet shuffled about. The soles of his boots stepped on the weapon.

The Prowler came to a gliding stop before the thick oak tree that was in their path.

Johnson flung open his door and ripped the seat belt free of his waist.

Russell unlatched his belt and retrieved the pistol as Johnson bolted from the idling cruiser. Russell squeezed the trigger without aiming, hoping to nick the deputy before he got too far away.

Two rounds popped off in quick succession, shattering the driver's side window. Johnson flinched and covered his head as shards of busted glass chased after him.

Max and Butch howled from the backseat. They clawed at the windows, begging to be set free.

Russell shoved his door open in a fit of rage. The deputy caught him off guard and got the best of him.

Son of a bitch.

A single mistake had altered his plans.

Russell wasn't a crack shot and struggled to get a bead on the fleeing officer who tore ass down the hillside. If he got too far away, Russell feared he wouldn't catch up to him, seeing as he probably knew this area better than Russell did.

The dogs.

Unleash the beasts.

Johnson kept rushing down the hillside. It was getting harder for Russell to keep him in sight through the thick shrubs and trees he weaved in and out of.

Butch howled and clawed at the window. His voice boomed like thunder.

Russell opened the door, unleashing the large cane corso.

Both dogs bolted from the backseat in a flash. They made a wide arch around the trunk of the tree and raced after the fleeing deputy at full tilt. Each canine sliced through the verdure at lightning speed as they charged after their target.

Once more, Russell was forced into the vast, lush wilderness of the Blue Ridge Mountains. At least this time, he wasn't alone.

CHAPTER NINE

SARAH

It couldn't be him, could it?

Spencer Laster, the Creeper, had tracked her down somehow within the madness that had consumed Boston. Sarah only got a quick glimpse of the man in the ballcap, but her intuition made her move just the same.

The mere thought of the Creeper being so close made her blood freeze. His coy smirk and dark eyes dancing over her body always sent a shiver down her spine. It was a disgusting sensation she never wanted to feel again.

Sarah ran hard and fast down the sidewalk, trying to put as much distance between her and the vile scumbag as possible.

Her stride was long, and her muscles burned from the stress, but Sarah didn't care. She pushed herself to the brink as she glanced over her shoulder.

She couldn't lay eyes on Spencer from down the empty sidewalk, but that didn't mean anything. He was sly and stealthy which made matters worse. She toyed with the idea that perhaps he was never there, and the undue stress, and lack of sleep and food conjured her deepest, darkest fear into reality. Her body was running on fumes, and a crash felt imminent.

Her purse slapped her side with each stride she took. Her Glock was spent and nothing more than a nonthreatening deterrent that would need to be refilled as soon as she could.

A voice whispered in her ears, low and subtle. She could feel the Creeper's tepid breath brush over her sweaty flesh, his fingers gently touching her arms and making her skin feel unclean.

She peered over her shoulder and caught sight of the ballcap flanking her and closing in. The bill concealed the majority of his face with only a deviant smile visible as he gained on her.

Panic consumed every molecule of her being as she surged ahead. She needed to give him the slip and do it fast.

Sarah skirted the corner of the building she was running alongside, and darted down the alleyway without breaking her stride. Her lungs stung, but she fought through the pain. She checked behind her for the Creeper, but didn't spot him on the street.

She continued her brisk pace, sprinting through the passageway in a dead heat.

Shouting and yelling echoed down the corridor up ahead. Sarah slowed to a slight jog. It sounded heated.

Sarah stopped shy of the bend as she gasped for air.

Flashing red and blue played over the brick wall to Sarah's left. It was the police which made her feel relieved, and also worried, considering the tumult that brewed from the adjoining alley.

Sarah toed the bend and craned her neck, searching for what threat waited around the corner. She struggled to catch her breath.

Madness Rising

She gulped down the large lump in her throat as she spotted two men fighting in the alley.

A cop and a civilian were in a heated struggle as they grappled with one another. Deep grunts and growls loomed from both men as they fought for control over what seemed to be the officer's sidearm.

"Stand down, now," the officer shouted while being driven back into the brick wall.

His attacker leaned into the uniformed man with his shoulder, then turned about while grabbing his wrists. With his back pressed to the officer's chest, he rammed his knee into the cop's arm.

The pistol discharged, firing off a single round that echoed down the alley. The sharp report and white flash from the barrel did little to deter the assailant's attempts at stealing the officer's weapon.

The scruffy man tugged and pulled at the weapon. He gritted his teeth and jerked his arms.

Sarah wanted to help, but wasn't sure what she could do. Approaching the battle could make matters worse since she was unarmed.

The men turned toward Sarah, giving her a brief glimpse of the officer. His face was twisted in an angry scowl. His teeth gnashed as veins bulged from the sides of his face and just above his brow.

Oh no.

Sarah knew that cop. It was David.

He was a family friend who had been there for her and Russell for as long as she could remember. He had helped them out when Jess was killed and when Russell was slugging through the depths of depression and alcohol. He was a good man, and she hated to see him in such a dangerous predicament.

Another round fired from his pistol as the thug knocked the weapon from his hand. It bounced off the concrete and slid away from the dueling men.

David shoved the thug off of him, putting some distance between the two of them. The man stumbled across the alley. He caught himself before falling to the ground.

The pistol was up for grabs. The thug went for the weapon as David rushed headlong at him. The surly thug grabbed the grip and spun on his heels, trying to get a bead on David. David tackled the surly man to the ground.

Both men grappled for control over the sidearm. She couldn't spot the weapon within the meld of entangled arms and bodies.

No one knew Sarah's weapon was empty except for her. She could help. Sarah pulled the Glock from her waistband.

She couldn't stand idly by any longer.

"No, no, no," David said, as he fought to redirect the barrel of the pistol.

Sarah emerged from the bend with her Glock trained ahead of her.

Another round chambered off between the two men. The flash of white was brief. David collapsed on top of the man.

"No." Sarah sprinted up the alley as David rolled over to the concrete. He gasped for air from the flat of his back while holding the pistol. His head rested against the pavement as his chest heaved in and out.

The footfalls approaching made him flinch, then he trained the pistol at Sarah. She threw her hands up and came to a screeching halt.

He squinted his eyes in confusion. "Sarah?"

"Yeah. It's me. Are you ok?"

Madness Rising

"Christ. What the hell are you doing out here?" David asked. "I could've shot you." He lowered the pistol and dropped his arm to the pavement.

Sarah tucked the Glock back in her waistband and kneeled down next to him. "It's a long story. You haven't been shot, have you?"

David lifted his head from the ground and cut his eyes to his chest. "I don't think so."

Sarah ran her hands over his dark blue uniform, checking for any injuries. Her fingers swiped through some blood, but she couldn't find the source. "There's some blood here, but I can't find where it's coming from."

David ran his hand over the dampness, then stared at the dark, red color on his palm. "I don't think it's mine."

They looked at the surly man who was motionless on the ground next to him. His eyes were closed, and he showed no signs of life.

"I'm just glad you're all right." Sarah stood up and offered her hand.

David took her palm and grunted as she pulled on his arm.

She helped him off the ground. It was easier said than done. He wasn't small by any means. Not fat, but more so stout and muscular.

"What are you doing out in this mess? I didn't expect to see you charging up an alley," David asked. He slumped over in a heap of spent energy while taking deep, hard breaths. His fingers ran through his damp hair as he exhaled through pursed lips. "It's not safe."

Sarah thought of Rick and that dreadful building. "I'm doing all right. It's been crazy and scary. I've come across so many horrible people, but was fortunate enough to have a few to help me out. I had a PI, Rick Stone, save my life. If it weren't for him, I'm not sure I'd be here right now.

David patted the dirt from his trousers, then said, "I'm glad you're ok."

Sarah glanced at the body. "What happened here?"

"This piece of work knifed some old lady a block over while trying to steal her belongings. I chased him over here."

A thin string of blood raced from the side of his temple to his chin. He looked haggard and tired, but at least, he was still alive.

David turned toward the man, then bent down. He pressed two fingers to the man's neck, then sighed.

"Son of a bitch." It was a grumble he tried to hide under his breath but failed to do so.

Sarah retrieved his dark navy duty cap from the ground, then offered it to him as he stood from the thug's side.

"Thanks," David said, with a defeated tone as he brushed his hand over the top of the cap.

"Is he–dead?" Sarah asked, staring at the man.

Her heart raced.

Sadness swelled inside of her.

Despite having seen multiple dead bodies since escaping the subway she had been trapped in, it never got any easier for Sarah to handle.

"Yeah. He's pretty dead." David placed his hands on his hips and looked at the body. "I'll have to radio dispatch to see how they want to handle this. The department is stretched razor thin."

He was stressed, that much was evident from the stern look on his face and flat tone of his voice. He shook his head and rubbed his hand through his damp hair before placing the duty cap on his head.

Sarah looked away from the bloody body, trying to focus. "Do you have any idea why the power crashed? Is this some sort of attack? I was on the subway heading to meet up with Mandy when the power just went out. I was stuck down there for hours before me and the other passengers decided to force our way out of the subway cars. When we made it to the surface, it was pure chaos."

David grimaced from the wound on his temple as he pulled the duty cap down on his head. He mumbled some choice words under his breath.

"Nothing official yet, but I've heard chatter that it was caused by a solar storm or something along those lines. Since communications have been offline, it's been difficult to reach anyone for more concrete answers or directions. The only thing we have that is somewhat functional is our two-way radios which are spotty right now." David turned toward his cruiser while thumbing the side of the receiver of his two-way radio that was fixed to his shoulder. Static loomed from the speaker.

He sighed, then rubbed his dirty hand over his face. "Communications aren't the only thing messed up. Whatever caused the blackout also spawned fires across the city on top of all the riots and other crap that we're dealing with. Emergency services are stretched razor thin trying to handle everything." He walked up the alleyway in a huff toward his cruiser.

Sarah flanked him. "Do they know when the power will be back on line?"

David shrugged. "No clue. Right now, we're trying to keep this city from ripping itself apart and burning down. So far, it feels like we're failing on both fronts." He skirted the open driver's side door and reached inside the cab. He retrieved the receiver of the radio and thumbed the button.

Sarah skimmed over the street, searching for any threats. She folded her arms across her chest as David shouted into the receiver of his radio.

"Dispatch, come in, over." he said, yelling into the receiver. "Say your last."

"What's wrong?" Sarah asked.

David held up his hand, silencing her.

A garbled voice crackled from the speaker as he pulled the receiver closer to his ear, trying to discern the transmission. He shot Sarah a quick glance, then shook his head in frustration. "But, sir, I've got a dead body here. I can't-"

David tilted his head, leaned against the cruiser, and listened.

People yelling grabbed Sarah's attention. It was coming from up the street at the intersection that wasn't too far away from where they were.

Sarah couldn't lay eyes on what was going on, but it sounded heated. Raised voices lingered in the air that morphed to shouting. She moved to the passenger side of the cruiser, then stood on the tips of her toes while looking over the roof.

A small crowd of people, maybe five to ten from what she could make out, were gathered out in front of a local convenience store. She narrowed her eyes to see what was happening.

David tossed the receiver back into his cruiser, mumbling under his breath. "Damn it to hell."

Sarah wasn't used to seeing him in such an agitated state. He was more of a mild-mannered individual who remained calm even under the most stressful situations. She had hoped some of that would rub off on Russell at some point over the years, but it never did.

"That bad?"

David scratched at the scruff on the side of his square chin. He glanced down the alley to the dead body with an unsure glint in his eye. "The department is calling all officers back to the station. Well, those of us they can reach. A number have skipped out to be with their families with all of the rioting happening. Some had to ditch their cruisers since they weren't able to refuel at any gas stations. No telling what kind of condition the vehicles are in now."

Sarah pointed at the small mob who had now taken to throwing any items of substantial weight at the storefront windows.

David turned away from his cruiser and craned his neck, watching the looters rush the store.

"Great." He shook his head, then turned back toward Sarah. "That kind of crap is happening all over. The longer this outage goes on, the more the civil unrest among the masses will grow, and it'll be harder to get things back under control."

"So, what are you going to do?" Sarah posed.

David pounded his hand on the roof, then said, "Get in the car. I'm taking you back to the station with me."

CHAPTER TEN

RUSSELL

Russell ran hard, trying to keep up with the dogs. They were hot on the deputy's scent, and were leaving Russell behind. He caught flashes of their fur dashing between bushes and large thickets before they vanished like ghosts.

"Butch! Max! Where are you?" Russell pushed through the low-lying branches while navigating the dense forest floor. Keeping the dogs in sight was challenging at best.

The dogs barked in response, but it was difficult to tell where it came from. It was low, and fading fast.

Russell tromped over the carpet of leaves and grass as he searched for the canines. Twigs, concealed under the blanket of green vegetation, snapped under his bulk. Subtle barks loomed from up ahead, but Russell couldn't pinpoint their position. He didn't want to stop, but he didn't know where to go.

Madness Rising

The farther he went, the more everything looked the same. An endless maze of rolling hills, rocks, and trees melded together in a dense landscape of beauty and death.

What I wouldn't give for the concrete jungle and some damn street signs, he thought.

It was jarring and confusing at best for someone who didn't know the area from a hole in their head. He jumped back into the deep end, and had to learn to swim on the fly without a lifeguard watching his back. Survive or die. Those were his choices now.

A burning sensation bit at the muscles in his legs. The uneven terrain of the forest floor worked on his sore ankle, from the plane crash he survived but a day or so ago, and caused him to run with a slight limp. Each hard breath he took stung his lungs with a vengeful bite.

Russell slowed to a jog, then to a slight stroll. He had to catch his breath, and give his body a moment to rest while he figured out where the hell he was going.

He panted, then doubled over with the heels of both palms jammed into the soft parts just above his knees. His head dangled toward the ground. Sweat dripped from his brow and splashed the tips of his boots.

It was déjà vu all over again. Russell was unprepared for a trek he hadn't planned on taking. There was no time to pick through the Prowler for any additional magazines or provisions. He had to move fast before losing sight of the dogs, which now, really didn't seem to matter, since they were nowhere in sight.

The officer's sidearm, and what wits he had, were his only defense in the wilderness. It wasn't much, but it would have to do.

Russell was out of his depth, but he'd manage the best he could. He had to. There was no other choice. Cathy's well-being rested on his shoulders, and he felt every bit of the weight crushing down on him.

That asshole is going to get it when I catch up to him, Russell thought.

Deputy Johnson forced him into a corner, and now he had to fight like hell to get out. The actions of the corrupt cop kept him from getting back to Boston. Back to Sarah, and hopefully, a new beginning.

Russell contemplated cutting his losses and letting Cathy fend for herself. He figured he could make his way back to the Prowler, then up to the road. From there, it would be easy to back track to Luray, then on to Boston.

But Russell wasn't cut from that cloth. Leaving Cathy at Mr. Wrights mercy wasn't something he wanted to do. He already had a laundry list of regrets a mile long. Cathy deserved much better than to be left to the whims of the local psycho. He was her only lifeline, and he wasn't about to let her down.

Damn itl.

Stress was building and adding to the already explosive mix that swam in the pit of Russell's stomach. Frustration crawled over him like spiders.

He hadn't paid it much mind in some time, or perhaps it had become second nature to him now where he didn't notice it, but his hands wouldn't stop trembling.

Russell straightened his back and breathed in. He closed his eyes and focused his scattered thoughts. He couldn't lose it. Not right now. That would be a death sentence for sure. His body was telling him that it needed a drink to even him out. Calm his frayed nerves. For now, his body would have to deal with not getting the poison, and hopefully, not punish him too harshly for it.

Madness Rising

A gust of wind blew through the canopy of trees, then downward across the forest floor. The loose leaves whipped about as the cool blast of air brushed against his sweaty face.

Russell ran the back of his hand over his brow. With a flick of his wrist, he craned his neck and searched for the best possible path to follow. He couldn't find any indicators that pointed to the dogs or Deputy Johnson passing through the area he was in which made his stomach twist in knots.

Great.

"Max! Butch!" Russell shouted for the dogs, trying to get a response from them. "Give me something here, boys."

A single bark rang out ahead of Russell. It was faint, but still loud enough for him to hear the noise. He took a step back and stood on the tips of his toes as he looked for the canines.

Another bark sounded off in the same area. Russell got back on the move. He raced toward the source.

Russell's fingers repositioned over the grip of the pistol as he skimmed over the area. His head was on a swivel, watching not only for the dogs but the deputy as well.

The cop was out there somewhere waiting for him. Russell knew it. Cutting his losses and leaving him be didn't seem like what Johnson had in mind. Russell was a loose end that needed to be dealt with, and couldn't be left to chance. What better place to take care of such a matter than the woods where curious eyes were nowhere in sight?

Russell whistled while on the move, trying to locate the dogs. He caught movement from the corner of his eye beyond a tree he ran past. A sharp bark stopped him cold in his tracks as his boots slid over the loose leaves.

Max rounded the trunk of the tree and galloped toward Russell. His tongue dangled from the side of his maw as he lowered his head to the ground.

Russell dropped to one knee and rubbed Max's head. The excited German shepherd licked at his face with a flick of his tongue. Russell took the loving gesture in stride, despite the foul smell that lingered from the dog's gaping snout.

"Where's Butch?" he asked. "Did you track down Deputy Johnson, yet?"

A smirk slit across Russell's face. It wasn't like Max was going to answer him back and carry on a conversation. Still, it felt good to talk things out even if Max didn't verbally reply.

The fur running along Max's spine stood on end without warning. His head sprung up and ears stiffened as he looked past Russell.

"What is it? You got the deputy's scent?" Russell asked as he turned to the side and followed his gaze.

The muscles in Max's body grew taut as low, muffled growls emitted from his throat. He took two steps forward and paused while scanning over the bushes and trees that surrounded them.

Russell squinted, trying to pinpoint what had Max on edge. He couldn't hear anything, and figured he must have picked up a scent or spotted something.

Butch barked, his deep voice booming like rolling thunder. It was intermittent at first, then became constant.

Max took off on a dime through the maze of trees before them.

Russell ran after the German shepherd, flanking the swift moving dog who weaved in and out of the plethora of trees without breaking his stride. This time, Russell didn't fall behind and ran harder to keep up.

Madness Rising

Butch continued to bark which Max honed in on without any problems. The booming call from the cane corso drew clearer with each stride they made. Through the trees ahead of them, Russell spotted Butch's dark fur.

Low-lying branches stabbed at Russell and raked across his chest and face as he shoved the gaunt looking limbs out of his way. Russell and Max tracked Butch, but there was still no sign of the deputy.

Max raced down the embankment to Butch who was pacing about in circles with his head trained toward the sky. He was at the base of a cliff that had vines and roots protruding from the wall of exposed earth. He gave Russell a quick glance as he continued to bark.

A bit winded, Russell stumbled down the slope. Butch trotted up to Russell, brushed against his leg, then turned back toward the cliff.

Russell rubbed the crown of the intimidating dog's head. He didn't bat an eye at the gesture. Russell skimmed over the dense, wooded area as his fingers scratched at the rigid body of the beast.

Butch focused on the top of the cliff. He stood on his hind legs while barking.

Max sniffed the area, then the base of the of the wall that was littered with mounds of rocks. His nose was trained to the ground. He'd pause, then lifted his front right paw.

Johnson had to be close, and Russell figured he was somewhere up on that ridge that overlooked the low-lying area they were in.

Russell took two hearty steps back and looked to the edge of the cliff. From his vantage point, it was impossible to gauge if the deputy was up there or not. He spotted no movement, but that didn't mean anything.

"You sure he's up there?" Russell asked while eyeing the barking beast. Butch kept his sights fixed at the ridge. Max surveyed the area. He was tracking something as well. "All right, let's check it out, then."

Madness Rising

CHAPTER ELEVEN

SARAH

David slammed his foot to the gas, sending the two-ton police cruiser barreling off the sidewalk and into the street. He cut the steering wheel counterclockwise, then pumped the brake.

The tires skidded over the pavement as the front end whipped about. He shifted from reverse to drive with minimal effort. The cruiser lunged forward, forcing Sarah into the seat.

A scowl formed over David's face as he checked the rearview mirror. He sneered at the mob ransacking the store, then shook his head in disbelief. "Jesus Christ."

Sarah peered into her side view mirror as the cruiser swerved from side to side. People ran from the stores and dispersed in every direction. She couldn't see what they had clutched in their arms as they fled the scene. "Nothing like a crisis to bring out the best in folks."

"Yeah. This has definitely shone a light on the seedier side of humanity," David replied. "Since I've been a cop, I've never witnessed such a decline in morality. Don't get me wrong, I've seen some vile things that would make your head spin, but not on a large scale like this. Most of what we've encountered the past day or so has been from the filth and scum that leech off the city, but like I said earlier, the longer the power stays out, the more stuff like that back there will happen. People are dangerous, more so when they are scared and unsure of things."

Sarah couldn't agree more. She had seen the lengths people would go to when the shit hits the fan. The dip in morality wasn't a gradual slope, but more of a drop from a steep cliff. The good she had come across paled in comparison. "I've seen my fair share of that scum. That's for sure. They've crawled from the sewers and taken advantage of what's happening. Probably why it's so dangerous out here right now." She shifted her weight in the seat as she tugged on her seat belt. The Glock nestled in her waistband bit into her stomach which added to her discomfort.

David cut his eyes to the firearm, then up to Sarah's face as she pulled it free of her trousers. "Is that why you're packing the Glock? I didn't think you got your LTC?"

Sarah glanced at the weapon, then set it in the seat next to her. "I got it sometime back. I could have sworn I told you. Anyway, it's normally left at the house, but I took it with me yesterday when I was on my way to meet Mandy. I thought I saw Spencer outside my place the other night. It put me on edge."

David rolled his eyes as he hooked a left at the intersection. "That nut bag is still bothering you? I thought the restraining order you got was working?"

Sarah shrugged. "I thought it was too, but it doesn't seem like it is. Actually, it feels like he's been following me. I've been catching glimpses of him here and there. I don't know. It could be the texts he's been sending me, which are disgusting at best, that have me on guard. I was going to come to the station after I hooked up with Mandy to speak with you about it."

"Why didn't you call me?" David asked. "Does Russell know what's going on with that creep?"

"Because I was planning to stop by and speak with you about it in person." Sarah paused for a moment, then continued, "Russell knows some about what has been going on, but I haven't told him everything. Just that I was handling it. Now that I think about it, I was kind of mean to him when we spoke. Haven't heard from him since. Then again, I'm not sure how I would seeing that there's no cell signal."

Static hissed from David's radio as chatter bled through the white noise within the speaker. "You know he's still in love with you, right?"

Sarah tilted her head, feeling much the same way about him, but she was scared of falling back into the same old routine that drove them apart. "I do. At the end of the day, I just want him to try. To get help to kick the alcohol and for him to talk to someone about how he's feeling."

"I've been busting his balls about it. When we spoke last, he seemed to be getting it. I think it's helped that he's been staying with Tim. I know Tim's been harping on him as well."

Sarah offered David a warm smile as she nodded.

"I'm just going to say that I think with all this craziness going on, and with that creep still bothering you, might be a good idea for you to have Russell come over to your place and stay. Just for protection and such."

92

"Even if I wanted to do that, he's out of town as far as I know, and won't be back until tomorrow sometime, if then. With all of the craziness going on, it's hard to say if he will. I don't know where he went or if he's even ok," Sarah said. "Just get me to Mandy's, and I'll be fine."

David cringed at the thought. "Are you sure that's the best place to be? Isn't she the one who knew that Spencer guy in the first place?"

"Yeah, but she didn't know he was going to turn out to be a psycho." Sarah respected and thought the world of David. He was a great guy, and she knew he was only concerned for her well-being. "Mandy's place will be fine. That's where I want to be right now."

A deep baritone voice barked over the radio. "Unit 2579, what's your status, over?"

David retrieved the receiver without hesitation and responded, "Heading back now as we speak. Just passed Mulberry and Jones."

"How are you fixed for fuel?" the gruff voice asked. "We've got a few units stranded. Their cruisers ran out of gas."

"I'm sitting on less than a fourth of a tank." The signal distorted, fragmenting the stressed voice on the other end. "Sir, you there? Say your last, over."

Static hissed from the receiver as David attached it on the main unit.

"Doesn't sound like those two-way radios are working too well," Sarah said.

David eyed the gas gauge while flitting his gaze up the street. He drove around the parked cars that sat in their way as he mumbled under his breath. "Here's the plan. I'll drop you off at Mandy's, although, I'm still not keen about, if you humor me and at least let me check things out to make sure it's safe. If I decide it's not, then the both of you come back to the station with me, all right?"

Sarah was strong willed, but she was also not blind to the dangers that lurked around every corner. Thus far, she had managed to take care of herself, but she was glad to get help. She might be stubborn, but she wasn't stupid.

"Just because it's you, I'll go along with it." She smirked at David who sneered in return.

"I'm glad you are. The next time I see Russell, I'll have to tell him that you broke down and agreed with me."

"You just had to ruin it, didn't you?" Sarah asked with a warm smile.

David chuckled as they turned down Ricketts Street. Mandy's apartment building wasn't much farther which made Sarah relieved. Being so cut off from her family and close friends didn't set well with her. She needed to know that they were safe and out of harm's way.

Sarah noticed a manila file folder wedged in the seat between David and the center console. Jess was scribbled on the tab. "You carry her file around with you?"

David glanced down at the folder, then said, "Yeah. I look it over on my breaks or when I'm following up on a lead."

"Mind if I have a look?" Sarah asked, pointing at the worn folder.

David rubbed his chin, then looked at Sarah. "A quick look, then you give it right back, all right?"

"I got it." Sarah took the file and opened it up.

A photo of a man's arm was clipped to the back. She studied the tattoo, bringing it closer. It looked similar to the one on the man Rick had taken down. Instead of the loops being a dark black, they were tinted with a light green.

Madness Rising

Sarah committed the green tinted tattoo to memory and closed the file. She stuffed the folder back between the seat.

David leaned forward in his seat, staring out of the windshield. They rolled past a cruiser parked in the middle of the street. The driver's side door was open, but nobody was present. The vehicle looked to be dead, powerless with no flashing lights or other markers to say otherwise. It didn't appear to have been ransacked, yet. Though, it could just be a matter of time.

"That Glock of yours is good to go, right?" David asked with a serious tone.

Sarah watched the cruiser as they continued on down the street, then said, "It's out. I've had to use it."

"What kind is it again?"

"A Glock 43. Don't you remember? You recommended it to me."

"Damn it," David said. "My police issued sidearm is a Glock 22. My magazines won't work with yours."

"Could you just give me a magazine like that if it did?" Sarah asked as she grabbed her piece from the seat.

"Yes, but I'd probably get in trouble. Not probably. I would."

"I had an extra magazine in my purse, but not sure what happened to it." Sarah placed her purse in her lap and opened the top. She sifted through the contents stuffed inside until she found the extra ammo at the bottom of the bag. "Never mind. I've got one right here. Guess I need to clean out my purse sometime."

"Good. If you do stay at Mandy's, that'll make me feel a bit better," David said.

"Are you not going to ask me why I had to use it?" Sarah really didn't want to dive into everything that had happened right then, but seeing that David was a cop and all, she figured he'd at least inquire about it.

"Not the time or place, but we will."

Sarah ejected the spent magazine and slapped in the fresh one with ease.

"Looks like you've grown comfortable with it," David said. "I remember how you were when we first went over the basics. You were a bit hesitant and timid even."

Sarah cycled a round, then set the Glock back on the seat. "A lot has changed over the past year. I'm not the same woman I was."

"I don't think any of us are who we once were," he added.

David pulled close to the curb of Mandy's building, then killed the engine. He removed the keys from the ignition and shoved them into his pocket.

The radio hissed, but no voices sifted through the white noise that loomed from the speaker of the unit.

"All right. Remember our deal?" David asked as he skimmed over the area around the brick building they were parked in front of.

"Yeah, I do." Sarah stuffed the Glock in the front of her trousers as David slung open his door. He stepped out of the cruiser and onto the sidewalk. Sarah followed suit and stood on the street.

His hand rested on the Glock that was secured on his hip as she skirted the front of the police car. She stood at his side as he walked toward the main entrance of the building.

David moved fast, but kept his eyes peeled for any threats. Sarah flanked him and stayed close behind as her head turned from side to side.

Ricketts Street was rather docile compared to other areas she had been in. The air still smelled of smoke, and the dull-gray haze refused to leave the sky, but that was about it.

Sarah couldn't spot much movement in the area which eased her troubled mind some. Perhaps looters and any other criminals had bypassed the area, or they hadn't arrived, but she tried not to think like that.

David ripped open the door and paused. He skimmed over the interior for a second, then moved inside.

Sarah funneled in behind him as they made their way through the long entryway. They passed the elevators and made for the staircase.

The glass doors at the entrance, and the two stacked windows above, allowed copious amounts of light to flood into the structure. It wasn't much, but enough to reduce the darkness within the building.

David took point and trotted up the staircase. His hand remained fixed on the grip of his holstered pistol as they neared the first floor. "Where is her apartment again? I haven't been here since she moved in."

"It's the second floor. Apartment ten B which will be to your right and at the end of the hallway," Sarah answered.

David nodded and continued up the staircase without breaking his stride. He hit the landing and swept the corridor. His hand slid over the banister while scoping out the vacant halls of the silent building.

A door cracked open across the hall. David turned toward the creaking hinges as he pulled his sidearm from his holster. A little boy's head poked out from the narrow crack as David lowered the weapon. An angry female voice boomed from inside as heavy footfalls charged the door.

"What are you doing, Blake?" she asked. "I told you not to mess with the door."

"But, Mom, there's a policeman out here," the young boy answered.

The boy was pulled away from the open door as she stepped in front of him. "Is there an issue with the building, Officer? Do you know how much longer the power is going to be out? Are we in danger?"

David held up his hand, silencing the tired looking woman. Her hair was a tangled mess, and she had dark circles under both eyes. "Ma'am, everything is fine. Just please stay inside."

She shot Sarah a peculiar gaze when she noticed the Glock tucked in her waistband, retreated back into her apartment, and shut the door.

They made their way down the hall to Mandy's apartment, which was the last room on the right. David had the Glock down at his side as they neared the dwelling.

Sarah grew anxious to see her friend. So much had happened that she needed some time to talk things out and to wind down.

She hadn't seen Rick yet which made her worry.

David stopped in front of Mandy's apartment and squared up with the door. He gave a single knock on the cream-colored door. They waited a few seconds in silence.

"Mandy, it's Sarah and David," Sarah said, aloud as she moved past David.

David tested the doorknob which was unlocked. He looked to Sarah, and said, "That's weird it's unlocked, isn't it?"

Sarah shrugged. "She may have forgotten to lock it or something. I don't know." She pushed open the door and peered inside.

The apartment was dark with the curtains drawn across the room. Light bled through the fabric and brightened up the room some.

David took point and moved inside as Sarah peered back down the hallway. Something didn't seem right, but she dismissed the feeling as nothing more than her nerves being rattled from everything happening.

The floor creaked under David's weight as he moved past the edge of the door. A sharp gasp fled his lips as he went limp and crumbled to the wooden floor. He hit face first. The Glock popped free of his hand as Sarah rushed inside to his aid.

"David, what happ-"

The door slammed shut behind Sarah as she dropped to her knees next to David's unconscious body. She gasped, then peered over her shoulder to the dark kitchen to the left of the entrance.

A figure loomed in the shadows. It was a man.

Sarah reached for her Glock as a *clicking* noise filled her ears. The man's arm extended in her direction as he trained the barrel of his pistol at her head.

"I wouldn't do that, if I was you."

CHAPTER TWELVE

RUSSELL

There was no easy way up the side of the cliff to the top of the ridge. Russell had looked for another way around that would get him to where he needed to be without burning too much daylight, and without risking life and limb, but he'd come up short.

Risking life and limb was a bit extreme, but that's how it felt to someone who never did that sort of thing.

Russell stared at the mountain of rocks stacked on top of each other and embedded into the side of the hill. It was the only way he could find up the side of the earthy wall. He shook his head.

The dogs would have to stay, but Russell hadn't planned on them coming anyway.

Getting up the side of the cliff was more than doable. He'd just have to take his time and try not to rush. The last thing he needed was to get careless and slip. A broken bone or internal bleeding would make this his final resting place.

Focus on the task at hand and why you're doing this, Russell thought. *Do whatever it takes.*

Both Max and Butch flanked Russell as he stepped in front of the boulders. The canines waited for orders as they stood rigid and still at the base.

Max nudged Russell's hand, and gave a slight groan to get Russell's attention.

"Yeah. I think it's safe to assume that you two are going to have to stay down here," Russell advised as he rubbed the crown of Max's head. "I don't see a way for either of you to come. The last thing I want or need is for my trackers to get hurt. Just stay put, and I'll be back down with the deputy before you know it, ok?"

Max barked as he licked Russell's hand.

Butch stared at him with an intense gaze before offering a single bark and sat on his haunches. He assumed Butch understood his command.

All right, then.

Russell secured the pistol in the waistband of his jeans. A couple of deep breaths, and he was on his way.

Slow, but steady, Russell climbed up the face of the boulders that were partially embedded into the cliff. The thick tree roots and vines that dangled like snakes offered a helping hand at certain spots.

Russell didn't dare look to the ground, but kept his focus on where he was heading. The dogs were pacing about the base. He could hear them crunching through the leaves as they barked in his direction.

His free hand grabbed at the vines close by and tugged, ensuring they'd hold his weight. There were few secure places to grab on the stacked rocks which made having the few vines that much more convenient.

He wrapped the green vine around his hand and pulled himself up to the next boulder.

Half way up. Not too much further.

He was making decent time for someone who never did that sort of thing.

Russell took a deep breath and paused. His hands and fingers were hurting. The muscles in his arms and legs were on fire. Doing such strenuous physical work hadn't been a part of his life for the past year. Not since he had stopped working out and focused on drinking as his new hobby.

He was out of shape, and his sluggish body made sure he knew that fact. Eye on the prize. All Russell had to do was keep the endgame in sight.

The toe of his boots wedged into a small gap within the mountain of rock as his free hand reached for an opening above his head. The tips of his fingers wrapped over the thin lip within the stone.

Russell pulled with his arm and pushed with his legs. The burning in his muscles grew more intense the longer he took. He gnashed his teeth and fought through the discomfort biting at his extremities.

The scant inch of rock under Russell's fingers gave, causing him to lose his balance. Fragments of the white stone crumbled away and sent debris down onto his face as he fell backward. His other hand held tight on the vine as it snapped taut, keeping him from plummeting to the ground below.

Dust filled Russell's eyes and distorted his vision. The tiny bits of debris wedged into the corners hurt and caused his eyes to water. Hard, panicked breaths spewed from his lips as the cold, boney fingers of death tapped his shoulder. His heart punched his chest non-stop. A large lump of fear clogged his throat.

Russell shook his head and ran his fingers over his eyes. He blinked, trying to rid the particles from each socket.

The vine was holding tough, but he didn't want to test its strength for too long. Russell tugged on the vine and pulled himself toward the boulders. He felt around the odd shaped rock and found another hold as the vine snapped.

The green, wiry, creeping plant fell to the ground at Max's paws as he barked at Russell from the ground. He stood with his front legs perched on the rock as both dogs howled and barked.

Russell took in another deep breath and blew it out to calm his nerves. His hands trembled, but he pushed on through the trepidation.

He scaled the remaining boulders at a snail's pace until he reached the top. The bones in each finger were sore to the touch and ached, as did the muscles throughout his body.

Beads of sweat raced from Russell's hairline down the sides of his face as he grabbed handfuls of the long blades of grass that grew at the edge of the cliff.

The salt filled pockets of spent energy slithered into his eyes and stung.

Russell grumbled in aggravation as he hoisted his bulky frame up toward the edge.

His vision was still distorted from the loose debris in his eyes. The dogs' barking echoed within the low-lying depression they were in and up toward Russell.

The long blades of grass held firm and didn't pull away from the ground.

Russell hoisted his bulk to the edge of the cliff, then tossed his legs onto the slanted hill. He rolled over onto his back panting.

His chest heaved as his lungs beckoned for air. He drew in deep breaths as he took a moment to rest.

Russell contemplated just shooting the deputy for being a pain in the ass, but he wasn't a cop killer, regardless if the dirtbag deserved it or not. Plus, he still needed him, which trumped any sort of dreadful end he had imagined for him.

The pistol dug into the small of Russell's back. He rolled to his side and retrieved the firearm from his waistband.

Russell flopped onto his stomach, then pressed both hands to the grass, pushing himself up from the ground. He rested on his knees and leaned back as he surveyed the area.

A number of large trees with bushes around their base concealed a portion of the area. More obtuse rocks blanketed the landscape which added more places for the corrupt cop to hide.

Where are you, you piece of crap? Russell growled under his breath.

He could hear subtle movements from the rich, green thickets before him. It was hard to discern if it was the deputy or an animal foraging.

Russell stood and huffed. He skimmed over the area, trying to get any sort of lead as to where to look first. Perhaps the dogs had been tracking another animal, and everything he had just done was a complete waste of time. Either way, he'd find out.

His nerves wound tight as he surveyed the area. The lack of alcohol swimming through his body caused the tremor in his hands to become more intense the longer he went without a taste. He didn't dwell on the withdrawals that were plaguing him. Doing so wouldn't solve the issue or help his current predicament.

The rustling within the thickets grew louder the closer he stalked. Both hands rested on the grip of the pistol as he swept the wooded area for the deputy.

Madness Rising

Loose branches on the forest floor snapped under his bulk. The breaking of the brittle wood was sharp and sounded much louder than he wanted. The rustling noise remained.

Russell squinted, trying to penetrate the dense foliage before him. Something was there, he just didn't know what.

One foot in front of the other, Russell moved closer to the boulders to his left as he closed in on the thicket. The endless places for the deputy to hide, just in the general area, made him feel uneasy. He was already at a disadvantage, seeing as the cop knew the area better than he did.

The movement within the bushes and shrubs ceased. It was instantaneous, as if his presence had been detected. Russell paused and scanned over the area.

He swiped his forearm across his sweaty brow as he trained an attentive ear for any footfalls close by. The wind howled and ripped through the canopy overhead, displacing the leaf rich branches. The canines' barking had reduced to a lull which was barely audible from where he was.

Russell pressed his shoulder to the rigid surface of the boulder and paused. His gut twisted in knots. The fine hairs on the back of his neck stood on end. He had a feeling the deputy was close, but he didn't know where.

He felt exposed, like a raw nerve that was primed for plucking.

Thunder rumbled through the cloudy skies overhead. The hint of rain loomed on the horizon—another obstacle Russell didn't want to have to deal with.

A squirrel materialized from the base of the shrubs and bolted past Russell's feet. He jumped back against the boulder. His finger squeezed against the trigger, but stopped before firing at the animal.

The light brown and tan rodent zigzagged through the grass. Its bushy tail stood on end as the small mammal skirted the rocks across from Russell. It slipped under the base of the boulder and vanished.

Russell shook his head and snickered.

Christ. Are you-

A blur flashed from outside of his view.

The deputy charged Russell at full tilt from the shrubs to his left. Lodged in his hands was a stout piece of wood that he lifted over his shoulder.

Russell flinched and took a step back while training the pistol at the incoming threat.

Johnson swung the branch with all his might. The pistol barked, firing off a single round as the dense plot of wood slammed into Russell's forearm. The blow knocked his arms to the ground, and the bullet went wide, missing Russell's leg.

Dirt kicked up from the ground.

The pistol fell from Russell's hand.

"You're a dead man, Cage," the deputy said, swung the hefty branch again.

Russell's arms throbbed as he ducked and lunged forward, spearing the deputy in the mid-section. A sharp huff fled the corrupt cop's lips as Russell drove him backward through the thicket.

Limbs and branches snapped as their bodies bulldozed through the shrubbery. Angered snarls and hard grunts swirled about the enraged men.

Johnson lost his footing, and stumbled to the ground with Russell latched onto his waist. Fists and elbows were thrown at any part of their torsos that were exposed.

Russell mounted the deputy for a split second before being thrown over his body. The world spun as he slammed into the uneven earth.

Madness Rising

Air ripped from his lungs. He coughed and hacked, then rolled over to his side.

Deputy Johnson pulled himself off the ground while coughing much the same way. The back of his hand wiped away the blood that trickled down from his busted lip as he loomed over Russell.

"You know what? I don't think I'm going to kill you after all." Johnson kicked Russell in the ribs. Russell dry heaved, then drew his legs up to his chest. "I think what I'm going to do is get my sidearm, blow out both of your knee caps, and leave you here for a mountain lion or bear to snack on. That way, you can think of the many ways I'm going to enjoy your wife once I track her down."

Johnson grabbed Russell by the scruff of his flannel shirt, and punched him in the face.

Pain lanced through Russell's face and stomach, as Russell's head snapped back.

His eyes clamped shut, and his body went limp in the deputy's grasp.

Johnson released Russell's shirt, dropped him to the ground, and backed away.

Russell could hear the deputy stomping through the grass, and breathing heavily as he searched for the pistol.

"Where did you drop my piece at, damn it." Johnson sifted through the tall grass, swatting the blades with his hand.

Russell had to move before it was too late.

The mere thought of Johnson even being in the same vicinity as Sarah made Russell's blood boil. His ribs ached and face throbbed, but that couldn't slow him down.

Blood and spit filled Russell's mouth. He spit the thick wad to the ground, then rolled over to his hands and knees. The motion ripped a subtle grunt of discomfort from his parched lips. He squinted his eyes and grimaced from the soreness in his ribs.

The melee weapon Johnson used to attack Russell was close at hand. The dark, rich brown of the branch was visible through the tall grass. Russell grabbed the bulky branch and dragged it across the ground to him as he stood up.

Johnson was hunched over, sifting through the grass while mumbling and cursing under his breath. His hands swatted at the tall blades as his frustration built to an explosive eruption.

"Damn it to hell," he said.

Russell stumbled through a narrow gap within the dense vegetation while wielding the branch like a baseball bat. Evil thoughts of bludgeoning the deputy to death right there in the woods coalesced in his mind. Bashing in his skull until there was nothing left except a pulpy mess filled Russell's thoughts.

His fingers wrapped around the large end of the branch. A scowl formed on his bloody face as the deputy found the pistol, and ejected the magazine. He wasn't the wiser that Russell was stalking him.

Johnson froze with the magazine in one hand, and the pistol in the other as Russell swung with all of his might. The wood smashed over the deputy's shoulder, knocking him forward. He dropped to his hands and knees. The mag and pistol vanished in the depths of the grass.

Russell glared down at the deputy as he struggled to get up.

"What? You want to kill me now? Is that it, Cage?" Johnson taunted.

You have no idea.

Russell shoved his boot into Johnson's backside, shoving him closer to the edge of the cliff. The deputy fell face first into the grass as he tried to crawl away from Russell.

108

Madness Rising

"Remember, you kill me and you'll never find out where Cathy is," Johnson said. "And all of this will have been for nothing."

A scowl took over Russell's face as he closed in on the back-peddling coward. The stick hung by Russell's side, the end dragging through the grass. Deviant thoughts of making the deputy suffer wouldn't leave.

Johnson stopped shy of the edge of the cliff, and a look of terror washed over the trembling man.

Max and Butch growled and barked from below.

"You know, I should extend you the same offer you did for me." Russell's voice was laced with indignation. His nostrils flared as his chest heaved. He peered at the cliff, then back to Johnson. "I could beat the crap out of you with this handy branch you found, then toss your worthless hide to the ground below. I figure you'll break some limbs, but survive for those bears and mountain lions you were talking about."

Johnson's lips trembled as he glanced to either side for a quick getaway. He rolled to his right and onto his hands and knees. Russell brought the business end of the branch down on Johnson's hand.

The deputy howled in pain as he dropped to the grass on his side while clutching his hand. He rolled to his knees, then sat up. Spit spewed from his mouth as he clenched his jaw. His face grew blood red and rich blue veins ran across his brow.

Russell placed the branch under the deputy's chin and lifted up. Johnson snarled. His nostrils flared like a raging bull. Saying he was pissed was an understatement.

Russell didn't care. "Let's try this again, shall we?"

CHAPTER THIRTEEN

SARAH

The shadowy figure loomed in the darkness of the kitchen—shadows concealing his face. The barrel of his canon remained fixed at Sarah's skull as he hovered over her.

"Toss that beauty you've got tucked in your waistband here," he said.

Sarah was lost, confused, and scared by what was happening. She had no plans of being at his mercy.

She reached for the Glock with a quick hand.

The mysterious man doubled down on her and said, "Easy there. Like I said, I wouldn't try anything stupid. I guarantee I can put a slug in your head before you could even think of firing off a single round, so don't test me."

Sarah grabbed the grip of her Glock while keeping her sights on the intruder. She wanted to know who he was, but couldn't get a clear enough view of his face.

Madness Rising

She pulled the Glock free of her trousers and tossed it at the man's boots.

From what little she could see, he appeared to have long hair that was pulled up into a man bun—something she hated on men. The hint of a beard caught her eye as well as he trained his ear to the wall.

Sarah glanced down at David, worried about how he was. He laid unconscious on the floor at her side. She nudged his ribs with her knee, hoping to get any sort of response from him. He didn't budge.

"Who are you, and what do you want?" Sarah asked with a slight tremble to her scratchy voice. "Where is my friend? What have you done with her?"

Man-bun smirked which was barely visible through the murk. He dug his hand into the front pocket of his jeans and pulled out a package of some kind.

The toe of his boot pressed to her Glock and scooted it across the floor into the kitchen, well out of Sarah's reach. He brought the crumpled-up package to his mouth, then cocked his head to the side.

"Did you hear what I asked?" Sarah asked.

The man shook his hand, then stared at the package. He made a fist, crushing whatever it was he was holding. "Yes. I can hear your incessant whining."

"Then answer me," Sarah said, as her voice rose an octave. "What do you want, and what have you done with my friend?"

Man-bun discarded the package on the countertop, then sighed. "First off, you need to lower your voice, and stop with all of the yapping. You're in no position to be demanding anything, Mrs. Cage. This can go one of two ways. The easy way or the hard way. I'd prefer the easy way, but I'm not opposed to doing what is needed to complete my job."

The man kept his piece trained at her skull. She peered up at him with a bewildered gaze.

There was more going on here than just a simple robbery. He knew who she was. Her stomach twisted in knots. She thought of Kinnerk, considering he was the only one chasing after her, but she never once mentioned her name or where Mandy lived to the goons who were after them. Not unless they somehow got to Rick and he told them. But that didn't make sense either. Since communications were down, they wouldn't have been able to contact Kinnerk.

Sarah's head swelled with confusion. On top of being scared, she was lost and didn't understand what was happening which frustrated her that much more.

"Listen. I don't know who you are or what you want, but my friend here is a cop, and I guarantee you don't want that kind of heat. Just leave us be, and tell me where Mandy is."

Man-bun didn't flinch or show any sort of worry. He seemed calm and collected which made Sarah uneasy.

"I don't know if you noticed the power being out and everything else going on, but the police have bigger problems at the moment. I wouldn't count on them being any help or coming to the rescue." He shifted the barrel of his gun to David, then said, "Just to be on the safe side, I guess I could snuff the pig here. Tie up any loose ends, so I don't have any added problems."

Sarah flung her body over David while holding her hands up in the air. "Wait, wait, wait. Please. Just leave him be, and tell me what you want."

"It's simple, really," Man-bun replied. "You come with me, keep that trap of yours shut, and I'll let your cop buddy here live. Either way, you're coming with me. The only question is whether or not I'll have to put a slug in the back of his head or not. That part is up to you."

112

Madness Rising

"You fire that weapon, and you'll have everyone on this floor rushing over here to see what's going on." Sarah didn't believe that, but she hoped that he would.

Man-bun snickered, and pointed at the hall. "That's true, and it would be a shame to have to kill them, along with your friend, but I will. Besides, it's not like they can call the police or anything."

He was right, and Sarah knew it all too well. His threat made her worry that much more. The lump of fear wedged in her throat choked her up as she forced it down and nodded her head.

Voices from outside the door caught Man-bun's attention. He pressed his finger to his lips while looking to Sarah. "Shhh. Be quiet, and don't do anything to get your friend killed."

Man-bun stepped toward the door and pressed the side of his head to the cream-colored wood grain.

Sarah remained silent and didn't make a peep as she got off of David. She sat on the floor, watching the man as he listened to the muffled chatter from the hallway.

He moved out from the shadows of the kitchen enough for some of the light that shone through the narrow opening within the curtains across the room to wash over his stern looking face. His black beard was neatly trimmed and cut close. His mocha skin was free of any scars or markings that she could see.

Sarah noticed something on his forearm. A tattoo of sorts that she couldn't make out. She stared at his arm, then flitted her gaze back to his face.

She thought of the Celtic Knot and Kinnerk's men. She wasn't sure if that was the tattoo on his arm, but she didn't want to find out.

Sarah's hand traced over David's duty belt, searching for the collapsible baton. She knew he carried one on him most of the time. The formidable weapon would do some damage.

Man-bun listened for a moment longer, then checked his watch for the time. Sarah's hand continued to trace over the belt until she found what she was looking for.

"Come on, come on," he said, under his breath as he twirled his fingers in a circle.

Sarah carefully pulled the baton from the duty belt to the floor. The darkness within the apartment helped conceal the weapon. She slipped it under her leg as Man-bun turned away from the door.

"It's about time," he said. "I really don't want to have to kill anyone today if it's not needed. That just complicates things. Makes it harder to complete assignments in a timely manner."

Sarah stayed planted on her back side as he motioned with his piece for her to stand up. He didn't have it trained on her, but kept it at his side and pointed at the floor.

Her heart beat like a snare drum. A surge of adrenaline spiked through her veins. She took her time in getting up.

"Come on. Hurry it up. I don't have all day here," he snapped.

Sarah glanced at David's unconscious body, then to Man-bun. The baton was clutched in her hand and positioned behind her lower leg.

He turned toward Sarah, then pointed at David's body. "You should feel good. You saved a life today. Bravo."

The tattoo on his forearm came into view and gave Sarah a cleaner look. She gasped. A shockwave of panic pulsated straight to her core. It was the same marking she had seen on the photo David had in Jess's file. The man who had killed her daughter.

A wave of emotions crashed into Sarah like a tidal wave. Her mind was drowning in a sea of emotions that caused her to panic and act on impulse.

Madness Rising

The man turned toward the door, offering his back to her. It was now or never.

Sarah removed her arm from behind her back and flicked the handle with a snap of her wrist. The wand telescoped out to a full-size baton.

The noise snared Man-bun's attention. He flinched, then jerked his chin toward Sarah.

She struck his hand that wielded the pistol. The weapon discharged as he lost his hold on the grip. The single round punched the floor near their feet. The pistol clattered on the planks of wood.

A venomous, spiteful scowl swept over Sarah's face as she continued to strike the man with the baton. She was angry and scared, and wanted nothing more than to exact a pound of flesh from the man who stood before her.

Man-bun held his arms up to deflect the punishing blows. Each hard strike from the metallic club smashed into his arm. He growled and knocked her arm down.

Sarah swatted at his thigh, unwilling to give up. He reeled back. A snarl fled his lips as he grabbed her arm and ripped the baton from her grasp.

"You're going to pay for that," he said.

Sarah dropped to the floor and went for the pistol next to his feet. Her fingers wrapped around the grip as he grabbed a handful of her hair.

"Get off me." Sarah pointed the pistol at the man's stomach.

Man-bun grabbed the barrel and twisted it from her hand before she could pull the trigger. He shoved Sarah backward toward to the middle of the living room.

Her feet tangled and sent her hard to the floor.

The back of her head slammed against the coffee table. Stars formed in the corners of her eyes. Sarah grimaced in pain as she rolled to her side.

Heavy footfalls stomped across the floor in her direction. Sarah tried to move, but was slow to respond. Her head throbbed and her vision blurred. She cradled the back of her head and tried to sit up.

The shadowy silhouette towered over her. He clutched the baton in his hand with a firm grip as he breathed hard through his nose.

"You just couldn't listen, could you?" he asked, angry and upset. "Neither could your friend when we picked her up. Guess your cop buddy over there is going to pay the price all because of you."

Sarah peered over to David and squinted through the pain that lanced through her skull. She thought she spotted him stirring on the floor, but couldn't be sure.

She closed her eyes and shook her head, worried that she had sealed both of their fates.

Madness Rising

CHAPTER FOURTEEN

RUSSELL

Johnson cradled his hand. He kept it close to his chest as he cut his eyes up to Russell. His body shook–sweat populated his brow and raced down from his damp hairline. Strings of spit clung to his chapped lips as he fought to control his anger.

Russell didn't bat an eye at what he had done. Choices were made. The deputy had gotten what he deserved.

"It doesn't look that bad," Russell said, with a harsh tone. "Can you move your fingers?"

Johnson's hand quaked. The flesh was a reddish color with lacerations running across it. His fingers twitched and bent as he grumbled in pain. "Yeah. Just hurts like hell."

"Consider yourself lucky, pal," Russell replied with a stone-cold expression. "I could've done to you what you were going to do to me. At least you can walk and use that hand. For now, anyway."

Madness Rising

Both Max and Butch continued barking from the base of the cliff. Their deep throated voices carried up the side of the exposed earth to the ridge.

Russell craned his neck and spotted the anxious canines pacing about with their heads raised to the sky. He waved his hand in the air, then whistled.

Max's tail waged back and forth as his tongue hung from the side of his maw. Butch looked pissed and angry, but that wasn't anything new. Russell figured that was his normal look considering his breed and from what he had seen of the large beast.

"Man. Those dogs really do hate you," Russell said, as he cut his gaze down to the deputy.

"Yeah, well, the feeling is mutual," Johnson shot back. "I wouldn't lose an ounce of sleep if either of those mutts caught a bullet or got hit by a car."

Russell didn't care for the harsh words spoken toward the dogs that had saved his bacon more than once. Without Max, he would've been torn apart and devoured by that mountain lion that stalked him through the woods after his plane went down.

"I'd imagine they feel the same way about you," Russell said. "I don't think they'd mind using you for a chew toy if I gave them permission, either."

Johnson scoffed, then rolled his eyes. "Whatever. They're not even your dogs. You might gain some ground with Max, but that cane corso is a different ball game. That mutt would tear your arm off if he was so inclined. I'm not the only threat out here and neither is the wild life. You'd be wise to remember that, city boy."

Whatever, Russell thought while listening to the babble spill from the deputy.

Russell grabbed Johnson by the arm and pulled him off the ground. A grunt of pain erupted from the deputy's pursed lips. He patted away the dirt and grass that clung to his uniform. Russell peered at his duty belt, searching for the officer's hand cuffs.

The steel restraints were secured in a leather holder on the far side of his waist. Russell reached around and pulled them out.

He shoved the steel restraints into the deputy's chest. "Put these on."

Johnson glanced down to the silver cuffs, then took them from Russell. There was no snappy taunt or quip offered from the disgruntled deputy.

The clicking of the ratchet teeth melded with the deputy's sighs.

The sound made Russell smirk. He searched the grass for the pistol and magazine as Johnson secured the cuffs around both of his wrists.

"I imagine you feel pretty good about yourself, huh, Cage?" Johnson's voice was thick with revulsion which didn't faze Russell one bit. "As I've said, this isn't going to end the way you think it will. You have no clue who you're messing with or what you are walking into. Best to cut your losses and head home to that wife of yours while you can. That window is closing with each step you make and will soon be gone. Besides, she probably needs you."

There was no doubt about that. Russell wanted nothing more than to be on the road heading for Boston, but leaving while Cathy was in danger wasn't going to happen, despite how hard Johnson tried to convince him otherwise.

"Save your breath 'cause you're wasting it," he said. "You just worry about yourself and getting us to where we need to be. You're not even close to being out of danger, so I'd tread lightly if I was you, bud." Russell swatted at the tall blades of grass for the weapon and magazine. He caught sight of the black casing of the pistol and the ammo within the depths of the vegetation.

120

Madness Rising

He discarded the dense branch and retrieved the items. Russell slapped the mag into the pistol and cycled a round. He turned toward Johnson, and motioned for him to move.

"Let's go. We're burning daylight here," he said.

Johnson held his cuffed hands up in front of him and deflected his gaze to the ground and away from the barrel of his sidearm.

"Do you know where you're going, or how to get back down from here?" Johnson asked as he walked past Russell. "That's a long way down if you lose your grip."

"No, but I imagine you do," Russell said, as he fell in line behind the deputy. He kept the barrel of the pistol trained at the small of his back. His finger rested on the trigger. If he tried anything, Russell wouldn't hesitate to fire.

Johnson skirted the boulders and followed along the narrow path that ran alongside the edge of the drop-off to their right. He didn't divert his gaze as they worked their way down the slight slope.

Russell peered over the edge. His eyes bulged, and he gulped from the height. He spotted the dogs following along at the base. They barked while staring at him, signaling that they were close at hand.

The deputy showed no hesitation in where to go. He traversed the uneven terrain slowly and steadily.

Russell's sore ankle ached, among other portions of his body that had been beaten down over the past few days, but it didn't hamper him much. The dull pain was more of a nuisance than anything else.

Besides, the last thing Russell wanted to do was let the deputy know that he wasn't a hundred percent or show any signs of

Derek Shupert

where he was injured. Doing so could put him at a disadvantage with the shifty cop.

They found a trail within the beaten down grass and followed it through the dense thickets. Birds chirped from the canopy overhead. The bushes they passed shook with activity from small animals that milled about the plants.

Russell's head was on a swivel. Any noise that sounded larger than a small mammal or rodent, he searched for the source. Johnson was right about one thing. They weren't the apex predators roaming the woods. Bigger threats loomed within the rich greenery that could be more deadly than them.

Johnson paused on a dime, then stood on the tips of his boots.

"What's wrong?" Russell asked as he peered over his shoulder.

The trail continued on down a steep slope that slithered through boulders and more challenging terrain. It wasn't as bad as when Russell scaled the face of the cliff, but it still had its dangers.

"This is our best way down," Johnson said, matter-of-factly. "It's not the safest, but it's also not the worst."

Russell glanced to Johnson, then said, "You managed it pretty well."

Johnson shook his head, then nodded to their left. "I came from over there. The terrain was much more even, and not as staggered as this."

"Then why aren't we going the way you came?" Russell asked. "I hope this isn't a ploy to try anything stupid, because that won't fly again."

He was already leery of the deputy, and paid extra attention to the moves he was making. Being at the mercy of others was one of the disadvantages of not knowing the area.

The deputy held his hands up in defense, then said, "We can go that way if you want, but it's going to take a lot longer to come around, and get back on track. This is more of a direct route to get down faster. Your call."

Russell looked at the deputy as he rubbed the stubble on the side of his chin. Fast or slow. Safe or not. Those were his options, and they sucked.

Time wasn't on Russell's side and he had already wasted more precious minutes than he cared to. Playing things smart was key to making it back to Sarah, but calculated risks would need to be taken. This was one of those moments that called for such a decision.

"We'll go this way," Russell said, while pointing down the rocky slope before them. Johnson shook his head, then sighed, but complied just the same. He took a step forward.

Russell grabbed him by the arm, stopping him in place. "Don't try anything stupid."

"You've made your point. I'm not going to try anything else," Johnson replied. "Contrary to what you think, I don't want to die out here. I intend on making it out of this alive. Besides, you're holding the gun, and I'm cuffed."

"Good. Just remember that when you get an itch to try something stupid." Speaking of being cuffed, Russell didn't think to ask for the deputy's keys which was a slip up on his part. He glanced down to Johnson's duty belt, then said, "Where are the keys for those cuffs?"

Johnson dipped his chin and shifted his waist toward Russell. "On my duty belt in the back. Near the pouch the cuffs were stored in."

Russell skimmed over the black nylon duty belt and found the keys. He pulled them off and crammed them into the front pocket of his jeans. "All right. Move."

The barrel of the pistol pressed to the small of Johnson's lower back—an added incentive to not try anything foolish. His word lacked merit, and Russell wasn't going to let his guard down, regardless of what the deputy said.

Johnson took his time, but moved with purpose down the boulders and narrow ridges of earth that acted like steps.

Loose dirt tumbled down the side of the boulders to the base where Max and Butch were waiting. The canines backed away and barked as they lowered to the carpet of leaves.

Johnson lost his footing and fell on his ass. Momentum kept him going forward. He panicked and shoved the heels of his boots in the soft, crumbling dirt to try and slow him down. His bound hands reached for the soil and grass. Wads of grass pulled from the earth with ease. Grunts of fright slipped from his mouth as he panted.

"Christ," Johnson said.

Russell crouched and grabbed the collar of the deputy's uniform before he was out of reach. His body stopped before dumping over the side of a boulder.

"Don't you let me go, Cage," Johnson said, scared and panicked.

"If I wanted you dead, I would've let you fall," Russell replied as he tugged on the deputy's uniform.

Johnson wormed his way to the left and fixed the heels of his boots in a nook. His body deflated against the rigid surface of the rock.

Russell took a moment, and gathered himself before nudging the deputy on the shoulder with his boot.

"Yeah, yeah," Johnson said. He climbed to his feet.

The remaining way down was void of any slips or mishaps. They hit the base of the cliff and breathed a sigh of relief.

Madness Rising

Max and Butch greeted the deputy with lowered ears and visible fangs. They stalked the corrupt cop. He stumbled away from the menacing canines.

Russell blocked their path, then held up his hands. "It's ok, guys."

He glanced over his shoulder to Johnson. There was naked fear in his wide eyes. The deputy wanted nothing to do with the dogs and feared their wrath more than anything else.

"You just keep them away from me, Cage," Johnson said, tripping over his words.

Max licked at Russell's fingers. His body relaxed and the growling subsided.

Butch wasn't as easily swayed, and kept his intimidating gaze fixed on the deputy. Deep growls loomed from the black beast's throat as Russell laid a hand on the crown of the cane corso's head.

The gentle touch that ran down the back of the canine's head stayed the aggressive dog. Russell scratched behind his ears which brought a groan from the maw of the hulking brute.

Butch huffed through his nose, then glanced to Russell. His long, pink tongue licked around the rim of his short snout, then flicked at Russell's face.

The pup's tongue slid across Russell's flush, sweaty face. "There you are, boy."

"So, what are you? The animal whisperer?" Johnson asked. His condescending tone wasn't lost on Russell.

"Not at all. I'm just not an asshole like you." Russell stood and turned toward the deputy, giving the unscrupulous lawman a snide look.

Johnson gulped, then relaxed his tense body. His arms lowered down to his waist as he exhaled a deep breath. He steered clear of the dogs who growled as he slid down the side of the boulder.

Russell flicked the pistol at Johnson, then said, "After you."

Johnson kept a vigilant eye on both dogs who watched his every move. He stumbled to the left and got back on the move.

Russell followed close behind with Max and Butch flanking him on either side. Any subtle noises that loomed from the trees or bushes stopped the dogs, but Russell stayed their urges to investigate with a stern tongue.

If Sarah could see me now, Russell thought. *She'd get a big kick out of this. Mr. I'm-not-a-big-fan-of-animals walking around with two following his lead.* It was a bit funny, and something he never thought he'd be doing, especially in the backwoods of Virginia. But here he was, making the best of a bad situation. At least the dogs were listening, and seemed to have taken to him. If they hadn't, this could've gone a different way.

Johnson kept a steady pace and made no snide remarks or attempts to flee. Russell made sure to keep a keen eye on the shifty deputy. Just because he hadn't tried anything, didn't mean the notion wasn't still nestled in the back of his brain. Russell was certain he was formulating a way out.

The day wore on as they trekked through the dense woods of the Blue Ridge Mountains. The sky overhead was cloudy with only brief spots of sunlight that broke through the clouds. The strident rays pierced the canopy in focused beams of light that shone to the forest floor.

A cool breeze blew through the trees, whipping the lush green branches about. The scratching sound of the limbs brushing against one another made the dogs' heads rise. They'd pause for a brief second, then lift their front paws off the ground. Russell would snap his fingers, then whistle, bringing the dogs back to his side.

126

Madness Rising

Sarah filled Russell's head. He wondered how she was doing. The uncertainty of not knowing ate at him.

He'd failed as a husband and father. He'd declined into a world filled of self-loathing, and drowning his shortcomings in whatever liquor he could find.

Despite his close friends trying to pull him from the depths of his own self-loathing, it took a catastrophic event to make Russell see the light.

Even with the world against him, and him battling his own addiction, Russell's plan was cemented in place. Find Cathy and get on the road. That was the objective. Do what was needed to get home to Sarah. Whatever it took, he was going to get it done and not let anything stand in the way.

Johnson paused.

"Why are you stopping?" Russell skimmed over the trees and bushes while keeping the pistol fixed on Johnson.

His face was flushed with sweat. He leaned against a nearby tree. The back of his head rested against the bark as his mouth slagged open.

"I'm tired and thirsty," Johnson said, his tongue dangling over his bottom lip. "We've been trudging through these damn woods and hills for hours. I'm just taking a moment to rest."

Russell was thirsty as well. His mouth was arid, gums sticky to the touch. He was getting dehydrated. Both Max and Butch panted hard with their tongues dangling from their maws.

The once cool breeze that offered a bit of reprieve had ceased. The air had grown stagnant, adding to the cumbersome trek through the foothills.

"I wonder if there's a stream close by or a lake of some sort?" Russell skimmed the dense, wooded area. He couldn't recall any such lakes or water sources when flying over the mountains, but he also wasn't looking for any at the time.

Johnson shrugged. "There are a number of small lakes and numerous streams that run through the mountains, but not any in the direction we're heading."

Of course not, Russell thought.

"How far out of the way is it?"

Johnson pointed to the east, then said, "If I remember correctly, I think there's a stream over that way. I don't believe it's too far from where we are now, but I'm not sure. To be honest, does it really matter? We need water or this little quest of yours is going to come to a grinding halt sooner rather than later."

He was right. The last thing Russell wanted or needed was to get sick from not having enough fluids in his system. His body was already punishing him for the lack of liquor in his belly. He felt nauseous, and continued to sweat more than he thought he should be.

The tremors in his hands remained and felt as though they had grown some in intensity. It was hard to tell if that was true or not since he found himself struggling to focus as the day wore on.

"All right. We head to the stream, lake, whatever, get some water, and we're back on the move right after that." Russell said.

Johnson tilted his head, then saluted Russell with two fingers as he pushed off the tree. "Aye, aye, captain."

The deputy's comment, and heavy indignation, wasn't lost on Russell. He didn't much care as long as Johnson did as he was told and didn't try anything else.

They hiked a bit farther through the rugged terrain that was filled with rocky, steep slopes and deep ditches. It was slow going at best, but there wasn't much choice in the matter.

A thought gelled inside Russell's head.

Madness Rising

What if Johnson was leading him astray and away from Cathy?

Russell curbed that thought, seeing as the deputy hadn't had any sort of fluids for some time. The amount of walking they were doing, and the sweat dripping from his tired face, he needed the water just as much as Russell did.

Johnson slogged up the rocky face of the hill. His movement was more lethargic and slower paced the longer they went. Russell was battling the same fatigue, but he had ample incentive to keep going, despite the lack of food and fluids in his system.

Both dogs raced up the hill past Russell. Johnson flinched as the beasts darted past him to the top of the hill. They stopped, and turned toward Russell and Johnson, panting hard.

"See. They're more concerned with getting some water than with you," Russell said.

Johnson didn't respond, but kept climbing up the slope to the top. Russell followed, but at a much slower pace. His legs burned. Every muscle fiber stung with each step he took. Both feet felt as though they were encased in cement.

"Man, and I thought I felt like crap," Johnson said. "You're looking worse as the day rolls on."

Russell glanced at the deputy as he dug his hands into the hard dirt and crawled the rest of the way. "Yeah, well, we had a car, but you messed that up, so here we are."

"I'm not talking just about that, cowboy," Johnson replied as Russell breathed heavily. "You're looking a bit green under the gills. Plus, that tremor in your hands isn't getting any better. Going cold turkey is a bitch. It would be a shame if you got too sick or weak out here away from any help."

Russell stood up straight, then shoved Johnson forward. "Move and keep the comments to yourself. You should worry more about your own wellbeing than mine."

Johnson stumbled as his boots raked across the dirt. He caught himself before falling face first to the ground.

"Hey, I'm just looking out for you, is all," Johnson responded with a smirk. "I am an officer of the law."

Sure. Whatever.

Russell didn't find the comment amusing in the least. He rolled his eyes. A few deep breaths to refill his tortured lungs and he fell in line behind the deputy.

Johnson snickered and continued on down the hill with Butch and Max following close behind.

The nausea Russell battled built with every second that ticked by. It wasn't much at first, just a slight annoyance, but the sickening feeling gained in strength. He didn't have the time or luxury to remedy whatever it was that made him feel ill with being out in the middle of nowhere.

He jogged down the hill and caught up with Johnson and the dogs who were standing in front of a large tree that had fallen across a gaping gorge. Max toed the edge, and peered down to the bottom, then backed away.

Johnson surveyed the log, then the gorge as Russell walked up next to him. "I hope you're not afraid of heights."

Madness Rising

CHAPTER FIFTEEN

SARAH

I t was darker now in the apartment than it was before. What little bit of light that bled through the curtains had lessened and cast the apartment deeper into blackness.

Sarah groaned in discomfort from her side. The base of her skull throbbed and ached. She winced in pain as she tried to lift her head from the floor.

A searing shot of agony punished her. Her eyes clamped shut. She didn't remember hitting her head that hard, but perhaps she did.

She took a deep breath, held it for a few seconds, then released it through pursed lips. Her eyes cracked open with a glassy tint to her vision.

David!

Madness Rising

A jolt of fear ripped through her body like a shockwave as she remembered Man-bun's threat of making David pay for her misdeeds. Her heart hammered inside her chest as her pulse spiked. Panic washed over her like a weighted blanket.

Sarah blinked twice, trying to clear out the haze that hampered her sight. Her head felt heavy as she forced it off the floor.

It was difficult to see or make anything out within the murk. She spied no dark mass within the space or on the floor near the entrance to Mandy's apartment.

David had been taken away by Man-bun. There was no trace of either one. For now, she was alone, and that didn't make her feel any better.

The guilt of her actions latched onto her like a leech. Each breath she took reminded her that David had probably taken his last. She didn't want to think of how he met his end. It was too much to bear.

Anger and rage swelled inside Sarah's body. She tried to press her hands to the floor, but couldn't. Her wrists were bound together behind her back with a zip tie. She tried to pull her wrists free, but the plastic chewed into her skin.

She rocked, struggling to sit up straight. At last, she managed to do so. The room spun. Her stomach churned. She sat there and took a moment to let the queasy sensation subside.

Sarah clamped her eyes shut, clearing out the subtle film hampering her vision. A wave of sadness crashed into her as she wept. Her head fell forward as Man-bun materialized from Mandy's room.

His menacing, ghastly gray figure loomed in the shadows and startled Sarah. She whimpered, then flinched as she leaned back against the coffee table. It scooted across the wooden planks, creating a boisterous sound within the silent apartment.

"You bastard. What have you done with my friend?" Sarah said, demanding answers.

Man-bun stood still and didn't answer. It made Sarah think that perhaps he wasn't really there, and she was having a mental breakdown. Imagining the whole thing.

"Your cop buddy has been taken care of. You can thank yourself for that," he answered. "We're not going to have anymore heroic acts or anything else that could jeopardize others that you care about, are we? Say, like your dear, sweet friend, Mandy."

Her face twisted into a scowl that was concealed by the darkness of the apartment. A swarm of emotions cumulated inside of her as she focused on the shadowy blob. Sarah wanted nothing more than to yell or tell him to go to hell, but didn't want to risk Mandy's life.

"No," Sarah replied.

Man-bun traced across the apartment to the front door. He leaned in close.

Sarah's head throbbed with a dull, nagging pain as she watched his every move. It made it difficult to turn her head without cringing in discomfort.

"As I said before, no one is coming to help you. When we leave here, and we are, you will keep your mouth shut, not make any sudden outburst, or try anything else. Am I clear?" Man-bun asked.

Sarah nodded.

"Am I clear, Mrs. Cage?" Man-bun asked again as his voice rose an octave.

"Yes, I understand." Sarah replied in a curt manner.

"Good. It's time for us to leave, now. Because of your actions, you have put me behind schedule and complicated matters. That, Mrs. Cage, will not do." Man-bun strode toward Sarah.

Madness Rising

She leaned back against the edge of the coffee table. Her body was tense, muscles taut as he reached for her arm. She didn't want to go, but feared Mandy being hurt, or worse.

Sarah leaned away from his hand as he tried to grab her arm. She knew better, but her body reacted on instinct.

"Mrs. Cage, I thought we had an understanding here," he calmly said.

Sarah bit her lip as she twisted and turned away from the man. Sharp, stinging strikes of pain lanced up through the base of her skull and filled her head.

Man-bun grabbed her arm and jerked her off the floor. Despite having her wrists restrained behind her back, Sarah pulled away and fought to break free.

"No. I'm not going anywhere with you," she said.

Panic consumed Sarah. She kicked at the man's shins. Each blow made him growl and move away.

Man-bun slapped Sarah across the side of her face with the back of his hand. Her head snapped to the side. A yelp fled her lips. She dumped over the couch in a heap of dead weight.

"Jesus Christ," Man-bun said, with a heavy sigh.

Sarah laid on the couch, trying to figure a way out of the mess she was in. She was a fighter, and not a victim. She would rather die fighting for her life than to go with him and suffer a much worse fate.

Man-bun grabbed Sarah's arm and yanked her off the couch.

Sarah was helpless to stop him or try anything else to get away. Her brain was mush, and her head bobbled about as if fixed on a spring. She couldn't think straight.

The brute's hands felt like stones–his grip was firm. The tips of his fingers dug into her skin. She feared more defiance would bring more wrath her way.

Sarah struggled to speak, but it came out as nothing more than pure gibberish. She could hear her attacker moving, but couldn't tell what he was doing.

He crammed a piece of cloth into Sarah's mouth. "This is just an added measure since you can't seem to listen and keep your mouth shut."

Sarah spoke through the foul-tasting fabric. It made her want to gag. It had an odd smell that she couldn't place, and she was afraid to try.

Man-bun bent over and retrieved the blanket from the back of the couch. He draped the soft cover over Sarah, concealing most of her frame. He grabbed her bicep and hoisted her body over his broad shoulder with ease. She dangled like a rag doll as he turned toward the entrance of the apartment.

Blood rushed to Sarah's head and made it pulsate that much more. It hurt like hell, but she feared that was the least painful thing coming her way.

The dizziness grew with each step he took. Her body swayed from side to side under the blanket. She was at his mercy, and could only wait to see what he had in store for her.

Madness Rising

CHAPTER SIXTEEN

SARAH

Sarah wallowed in a mixture of emotions as she rocked back and forth. The blanket was still draped over her body, hiding the outside world from her view. It felt like she was in a car from the sounds that filled her ears and the rigid surface she was lying on. The grumble of the engine, squealing tires, and the hissing of the radio bleating from the speakers in the door near her head indicated as much.

The piece of fabric crammed into her mouth had been removed, giving her a reprieve from the bad taste that filled the fibers. Sarah licked around her lips; they were dry and coarse. The inside of her mouth was just as arid.

Her hands were still bound by the zip ties that cut into her wrists. Any subtle shift of her arms to try and slip free stung and caused her pain.

Madness Rising

Sarah's jaw felt swollen from the backhand she received from Man-bun. Opening and closing her mouth hurt and made her wince. The only saving grace was the haze coating her eyes had waned, and she could see without things being blurred or distorted.

The blanket covered only a portion of her head. Light seeped in from around the edge just above her brow. Sarah wiggled her fingers, trying to capture a portion of the fabric between the digits. Her nails snagged the soft, plush blanket. She pulled the dense cover away from her head as she craned her neck. More light became visible as the blanket slipped past her eyes, then her nose. Wild strands of hair dangled in front of her face. Sarah huffed, then blew to clear the obstruction.

She squinted as her eyes adjusted to the light. Rocking her head back and forth, to help in removing the hair from in front of her face, only made the discomfort swell inside her skull.

Sarah pressed the side of head to the backseat and closed her eyes as the nagging pain persisted. She focused on trying to find a way out of her current situation as the torment subsided.

Man-bun fiddled with the radio, trying to find a station that wasn't drowning in white noise. His fingers pressed the digital buttons and looped through the endless stations without stopping.

The way his arm was situated, Sarah got a better look at the tattoo which only reaffirmed what she thought she saw inside the dark apartment. The Celtic branding on his flesh told the tale, but she didn't know how it all connected. From Jess's death, to Kinnerk's goons, and now to Man-bun. They were all links in an ever-growing chain that was tightening around her body.

She continued to move her arms up and down while keeping a watchful eye on her abductor. Wetness coated her hands and forearm as a searing twinge tore through her arms. The plastic was biting into her flesh. Despite the discomfort, she fought on.

Derek Shupert

It was hard to gauge where they were heading. All she could see through the front windshield was the gray, cloudy sky. A random signal and street sign flashed before it vanished. She couldn't make out the verbiage fast enough.

Through the back passenger side window, the tops of buildings passed by which didn't offer any additional help.

Man-bun turned his head to the side, then dipped his chin as he worked the steering wheel. Sarah stopped moving her arms and stared at him. She got a better look at his face in the daylight.

His skin was a mocha brown with a nicely trimmed black beard. His black hair was pulled tight with no wiry hairs visible. The one difference she did notice was a small scar on the right side of his cheek.

"Well, look who's stirring back there," he said, with a wiry grin. "I took that gag out of your mouth. Didn't need you suffocating or anything like that. Just needed to keep you silent until we got out of the building and into the car."

Sarah disregarded everything he said. She stared at him. Short and curt, she asked, "Where are you taking me?"

Man-bun faced front and center, but glanced at her from the rearview mirror. "Well, you'll find out soon enough as long as this mess of stalled cars doesn't slow us down. I'd be willing to bet that the majority of them ran out of gas since the pumps aren't working. Fortunately, I fueled up before the power went out. Lucky, I guess."

Small talk. Really?

Sarah didn't care about what Man-bun was saying. He didn't answer her question, so his words fell on deaf ears. Sitting there, a thought gelled inside her head. He had thrown her in the back seat instead of the trunk. She was glad and all, but it just seemed like a high risk considering he was kidnapping her.

Madness Rising

"I'm curious, why didn't you put me in the trunk?" Sarah posed. "Seems to me that you're at a big risk of getting caught if we have to stop."

The smile remained on his face as he snickered under his breath. "You're still clinging to that razor thin piece of hope, aren't you? When I carried your body from that apartment, do you know how many people tried to help you? None. Zero. Zilch. That's how many. I have no doubts that any who might have witnessed what was happening wanted to, but fear has it's place, especially when you can't call for help."

Sarah rolled to her right and continued trying to free her wrists. She hoped Man-bun wasn't the wiser. Listening to him speak, he seemed confident that he was in the clear and had the upper hand.

"That's a pretty cavalier attitude to have," she said. "I mean, what would happen if I flipped over onto my back and busted out this side window. I think someone, maybe even a cop, would be wondering what was happening."

Man-bun nodded, but still, he didn't seem concerned. "That is true. Someone might wonder what's going on and try to interfere, which, to be honest, wouldn't end well for them. After all, you already have a body count going by trying to be a hero and not following the rules. I would say ask your cop buddy, but, oh yeah, he's dead."

Sarah snarled at the snide comment. It boiled her blood, and made her that much more determined to break free.

"I'm sure you've seen the state of the city," he said. "The police have bigger matters on their hands and as of right now, what I'm doing is at the low end of the totem pole. We've already had this discussion, but I do commend you for trying to throw me off my game."

"You know, I've known guys like you my entire life. Cocky, arrogant, and everything in between. Thinking they could do what they wanted, and no consequences would come crashing down on them. Eventually, it does happen. Mark my words," Sarah said.

Man-bun honked his horn, then stepped on the gas. The engine revved as he wrenched the steering wheel clockwise. He threw his hands up in the air, then offered the middle finger to some unlucky soul.

"Damn people," he said, shaking his head. "Would you like to know the main reason why you won't try anything stupid or hasty?"

"Please, enlighten me," Sarah said.

"You're friend, Mandy. It would be a shame if something happened to her as well because you couldn't shut up and behave," Man-bun replied. "I know you're hardheaded and all, but you are also smart."

Sarah wasn't sure she wanted to gamble with Mandy's life. Not after what happened to David. She couldn't bear another death on her conscience.

She stowed any grand idea's of trying to alert any passersby.

Man-bun's coy smile remained as he tilted his head. His overwhelming confidence in himself gushed from his every pore which made Sarah sick to her stomach.

What a piece of crap.

"You know, we've met before," he said, after a few moments of silence. "I thought I made more of a memorable impression, but I guess I didn't."

Sarah's face scrunched in confusion as she stared at him. "I don't recall us meeting. Though, that tattoo on your forearm has been popping up a lot."

The car jolted, shifting Sarah in the seat. It felt like they ran over something, but she couldn't be sure. She hoped it wasn't a person. Considering his proclivity to killing, she wouldn't put it past him.

Man-bun glanced at the tattoo on his arm. "Yeah, I guess you wouldn't remember my face that night since it was covered up. I thought I had my tattoo covered up good enough. Guess I didn't."

"That night?" Sarah parroted his words. A sickening feeling rooted in her stomach, and ran through the rest of her body. Only one event came to mind.

"Yeah. It was about a year or so ago. I can't remember exactly when. I'm not good with dates and all."

Sarah's eyes glassed over with tears as a wave of emotion crashed into her. That fateful night replayed in her head as she relived each second of the torment.

Sadness, anger, and loss ran down her cheeks without pause. She couldn't help it, or stop the flow as she stuffed her face into the seat.

Her head cocked to the side. "Tell me why you broke into my house? Why you took my little girl from me? Why you destroyed my marriage and life? Because of you, I have lost everything. You took that from me."

Man-bun's smirk evaporated in a blink. An emotionless void washed over his face as he nodded. "I understand you're angry and confused. That was not how things were supposed to go down that night."

"What does that even mean?" Sarah asked. Her arms pulled harder against the zip ties. She no longer cared if he could see what she was doing or not. Sarah wanted to be free of the restraints. To wrap her hands around the spineless man's throat for what he had done and choke the life from his body. She wanted to look into his eyes as those last gasps of air fled from his mouth, so he could feel the same helplessness that she had.

The terrain changed. A clicking sound played inside the car. It sounded like they were driving over wooden planks. Perhaps over the dock. Sarah wasn't sure, though, if that's where they were, or if that's what she was even hearing.

Man-bun kept his attention focused out of the front windshield. They drove a bit longer before the car came to gradual stop. He placed the vehicle into park and killed the engine.

"Are you not going to answer me?" she asked.

He twisted in his seat and peered back at Sarah. His face was stone cold. "I'm sorry, but our time together has come to an end, Mrs. Cage."

He glanced out of the back-passenger window and nodded. The door flew open. Sarah gasped as she jerked her chin toward the open door. A man stood just beyond the car. He grabbed Sarah's ankles and yanked her toward him.

Sarah yelled and kicked her legs, trying everything she could to stop what was coming.

The burly man held her close, dragging her away to an uncertain future.

CHAPTER SEVENTEEN

RUSSELL

Russell's eyes widened at the sight of the cavernous fissure before him. Heights were not his thing, and something he avoided if at all possible. This was one of those moments that he wouldn't be able to steer clear of, even if he wanted to.

Water was their immediate mission. They all needed it. Russell had to trust that Johnson knew where he was going, and that he wasn't leading them away from Cathy or into a trap.

"You know, we can always turn around and go back the way we came," Johnson said. "Might take us longer to find water, but I imagine we'll run into some sooner or later. Your call."

Russell didn't want to backtrack, but he also wasn't keen on crossing the less than desirable log. The wood looked brittle and rotted. White splotches covered the immense tree trunk at random spots. It did little to stay his nerves.

His palm rubbed over his face as he took in a gulp of air. The nauseous feeling and light-headedness wouldn't leave him be. He exhaled a single deep breath and bent down.

"You're sure it's safe to cross?" Russell asked while grabbing a handful of bark that snapped off into his hand.

The crumbling wood slipped through Russell's fingers as he glanced up to the deputy.

"I think it will hold us, but not all of us at one time," Johnson said.

He shoved his boot against the jagged ends of the trunk. The tree didn't move or shift, then again, Russell didn't figure it would from him nudging it the way he was.

"Are you suggesting we go one at a time?" Russell asked as he raised his right brow.

Johnson shrugged. "Well, yeah. That, or I figure we can go two at a time. A dog with each of us. That way, the weight is equally distributed."

Russell peered down to Max and Butch who were sniffing the ground close by. Having Johnson go by himself wasn't an option that Russell liked. If Johnson tried to run once making it across, Russell wasn't confident he could hit a moving target. Plus, with all of the trees, bushes, and tall grass on the other side, he could disappear fast.

"Fine. We'll go two at a time. Butch can go with you, and I'll take Max," Russell said.

"Like I said, it's your call." Johnson looked to the black beast, then nodded. A naked fear lingered in his eyes, but getting water and surviving trounced any hesitation he had.

Johnson stepped up onto the log. When Russell grabbed his arm, Johnson dropped back down to the ground and looked at him.

Madness Rising

"Don't try anything stupid. You get across and you wait for us to come over. You got it?" Russell asked.

"Yeah. I got it," Johnson replied.

He stepped back up onto the log as Russell whistled for the dogs. Both Butch and Max bolted from the nearby bushes and ran toward them.

"I suppose I couldn't persuade you to remove the cuffs, could I?" Johnson inquired while presenting his hands to Russell.

"Not a chance in hell," Russell said.

Johnson faced forward and headed down the tree trunk. Slow and steady, he kept to the center of the log as he looked down to his feet.

Russell bent down and looked at Butch. "Keep an eye on him until we come across, will ya? If he gets out of line or tries to run, bite him."

Butch licked around the rim of his maw as he glanced to the deputy.

"Yeah. The guy you dislike more than me," Russell added.

Butch groaned and turned toward the log.

Russell patted his hand on the bark, signaling for the cane corso to move.

Butch hoped up on the end of the trunk and paused. He glanced to Russell with a stern, focused look. His clipped ears twitched from the numerous bird sounds and other animals in the area.

"It's ok. We'll be right behind you." Russell felt stupid talking to the animal as he was, but it made him feel as though he wasn't alone. The deputy didn't count.

Butch faced forward, then trotted down the log. Flanking the deputy, he caught up fast and stalked him.

Johnson continued moving with Butch at his six.

147

Russell watched the tree trunk for any shifts or hints of the wood giving from their bulk. He stepped to either side of the log and focused on the middle portion. It appeared to be holding together with no signs of the wood breaking. Although relieved, he still wasn't keen on going across the log, but he had to man up and face his fear.

Johnson made it to solid ground with Butch following close behind. They stepped away from the log and turned toward them.

"Are you ready to do this?" Russell asked Max. The German shepherd groaned while resting on his haunches. He sprung up and waited for his handler to give orders.

"Looks like you're more ready than I am." Russell took the lead and mounted the trunk. His heart raced and palms sweated from the thought of walking across the log. He told himself to just do it and not look down. Sarah and Cathy were counting on him. He couldn't flake out now.

One precarious step in front of the other, Russell held his arms out to either side of him to stable himself. The dizziness that had latched onto him made each step feel like he was going to dump over the side of the trunk.

The farther he moved out, the harder his heart punched his chest. Quick breaths fled his lips. He fought to keep control of the fear that was trying to get him to look down.

Max flanked Russell and matched him step for step. The Shepherd didn't bark or try to skirt around him. He waited patiently and moved when he was able.

Halfway there, Russell thought as the sight of solid ground gave him added incentive to keep moving.

Snap.

"What the hell was that?" Russell asked in a panic.

Madness Rising

He acted upon instinct and glanced down to his feet. The fissure below him filled his gaze and sent a surge of dread that washed over him.

Russell froze, unable to move as the cold, boney fingers of death reached up from the ground and grabbed his ankles. Butch barked from the sidelines while racing back and forth near the end of the log.

"I'd move. Sounds like it's about to give," Johnson said, motioning to Russell to get going.

The wood popped and creaked, acting as though it would give at any moment.

Russell forced his feet to move as he headed for safety. His boots sunk into the spongy surface through the bark. Crackles and pops filled his ears as the log shifted.

Russell jumped while on the run, diving for the edge of the cliff. He hit hard, flat on his stomach, and rolled across the ground. The air burst out of him as he came to a stop.

The trunk snapped in half. Both pieces vanished from sight. Russell breathed in while trying to speak. "Max. Max."

His voice was strained and hoarse. He glanced about worriedly.

A wet tongue flicked over Russell's ear from behind. He flinched and leaned away.

Russell twisted, relieved at the sight of Max standing beside him. "Oh, thank God. Cathy would've killed me if anything happened to you." Russell patted Max's head, then ran his fingers over his coat as he stood up.

Max licked at the end of his fingers, then ran over to Butch.

"You're one lucky son of a bitch, Cage," Johnson said.

"I guess you could say that," Russell countered while wiping the dirt from his pants.

149

He was shaken from nearly dying, but held himself together as best he could.

Both dogs froze. Their ears stood on end.

"What is it, guys?" Russell inquired as he looked over the dense trees and foliage around them.

"It's probably just a rabbit or squirrel," Johnson advised while leaning in close to Russell. "We are in the woods after all, and they are predators."

The dogs searched the surrounding area as low growls loomed from their throats. Muscles rippled in Butch's chest as he took a step forward. Max lowered his head and sniffed the ground before looking back up.

"I don't know. Doesn't feel like a rabbit or squirrel from the way they're both growling," Russell said, in a whisper.

The sound of branches snapping silenced the group. Growling from the dogs grew in volume as they turned to the north. Butch bared his fangs, then lowered his head.

Max took a step forward.

"No. Stay," Russell said.

Max paused, but kept growling.

Butch inched forward a bit more before complying.

A man materialized twenty paces from the trees to their left, wielding a rifle. Both Max and Butch barked and growled, but stayed put. They were antsy and wanted to charge, but obeyed Russell's command.

The man lowered his rifle, then craned his neck. Russell couldn't get a clear view of his face from the camo hat that was pulled down low over his head.

The man's green and brown camo jacket blended in with the nearby scenery as he looked their way. He clutched the rifle close to his chest as he approached with caution.

"Crap," Johnson said, under his breath, diverting his gaze to Russell. He whispered in his ear, "I know that guy. He's one of Marcus's men."

Russell reached for the pistol tucked in his waistband as Johnson grabbed his wrist. "What?"

"Just hold on. He's a crack shot with that rifle, and unless you're one hundred percent sure you can hit him, I wouldn't do it. Not until he gets closer. You miss, and he'll drop you in a heartbeat, and maybe me. I don't know," Johnson said.

"Fine. I'll wait." Russell eyed the hunter coming toward them, and removed the pistol from his waistband. He held it behind his back with his finger over the trigger.

"Let me do the talking. I'll see if I can get us out of this," Johnson said, in a low tone.

Russell glanced to the handcuffs on the deputy's wrist. "That's going to be a hard sale considering you're cuffed. He's going to know something's up, if he doesn't already."

"Just chill and let me speak to him, all right?"

"Play it smart," Russell said, warning the deputy.

"Brian, what in the hell are you doing way out here in the middle of the woods, especially in your uniform?" the man asked.

Johnson kept his arms down around his waist. The tall blades of grass around them barely concealed the restraints. "It's a long story, Pete. Is Tony out here with you?"

"Who the hell is Tony?" Russell asked as he watched Pete's every move.

"His hunting buddy. They normally hunt together. So, if one's out here, odds are the other isn't far behind," Johnson replied in a whisper.

Great.

"Yeah. He's somewhere out here," Pete answered without giving any more details. He eyed Russell, then spotted the agitated dogs. "Who's your friends?"

Butch and Max continued to growl, stopping the burly man in his place. He honed in on the anxious animals. His fingers repositioned over the rifle as he held it close. His body tightened as his tongue slid over his lips.

The dogs didn't advance, but Russell wasn't sure how much longer Butch was going to obey. He was headstrong and could lash out at any moment. The longer this went on, the bigger the risk of a shootout.

"Oh. Just a friend is all," Johnson answered, calm and collected.

Pete looked suspiciously at Johnson, then dipped his eyes toward the grass around his wrists. He glanced to Russell as both hands twitched over the rifle. "What's going on here, Brian? From here, it looks like you're wearing handcuffs."

Tension swarmed among the men. Pete gulped. Both dogs continued to growl, asserting their dominance, and letting the stranger know he was being watched.

Russell couldn't let Pete leave. Not now. He couldn't risk him running to Marcus or alerting his friend. He had to take him out, but wanted to avoid discharging his weapon if at all possible.

Pete hesitated a moment longer, then brought the rifle to bear.

Russell pulled the pistol from behind his back. A round was already chambered and ready to rock.

"Whoa, whoa," Johnson said, as he lifted his hands into the air. "Let's just calm down here, all right."

Pete trained his rifle at Russell, then Johnson. "Brian, you better start talking now. What the hell is going on here?" The dogs barked and growled louder, inching toward the threat.

Madness Rising

"Just put-"

"Lower your rifle, now, or I will shoot," Russell said. "I don't want to shoot you, but I will if you don't lower your weapon."

The buttstock of the rifle stayed pressed to Pete's shoulder. The wild strands of his thick, black beard dangled over the wood grain of the stock as he shifted his gaze among the threats before him.

The radio fastened to Pete's hip crackled. Butch took off in a dead sprint toward the hunter. Pete turned to the black beast. Russell pulled the trigger, discharging the pistol.

Fire spat from the barrel, followed by a sharp report that echoed throughout the dense forest. Pete squeezed the trigger of his rifle as he turned toward Butch.

Johnson flinched, then covered his head as he darted off to the right. Pete's round struck the deputy, sending him tumbling to the ground.

Russell's round hit Pete in the torso, knocking him off balance as Butch closed in on the falling man.

Russell kept the pistol trained in Pete's direction as he collapsed within the tall grass. He glanced over to Johnson. Russell couldn't tell at first where the deputy had been shot or how bad it was.

"Christ." Johnson bellowed in pain. "That son of a bitch shot me in the leg. Ahh."

Butch attacked Pete in the depths of the tall grass. He could hear the groans of the hunter, followed by the screams of pure terror.

"How bad is it?" Russell asked as he inched toward Pete.

"I don't know. It hurts. That's how bad it is, Cage," Johnson answered.

"Keep pressure on it or whatever. I'll be right back," Russell said.

"Where are you going?" Johnson called out bewildered.

"To check on your hunter friend."

Russell panted and blinked twice as he surged through the grass. Adrenaline spiked through his veins as he closed in on the pitiful pleas of the hunter.

Pete was prone on his back with Butch off to his side. The rifle lay in the grass next to his body as he tussled with the cane corso.

Butch had Pete's forearm wedged in his mouth as he growled and jerked his head. Pete cried out.

Max flanked Russell, but didn't engage the hunter. He growled and barked, then paced back and forth.

Russell kicked the rifle out of Pete's reach. The barrel of the pistol zeroed in on Pete's chest as Russell towered over the injured man.

Pete winced and fought to pull his bloody arm free of Butch's vise-like hold, but the wound in his chest kept him from being able to do so. He groaned in agony. Pete's face was flushed with beads of sweat that bubbled on his brow.

"Butch, that's enough," Russell said, at the growling black beast.

His command fell on deaf ears. Butch continued wrenching his head and tugging at the mangled limb, acting as if he wanted to rip it clean from the man's body.

Russell lowered his pistol and stepped over Pete's fluttering legs. Engaging Butch at that moment didn't feel like a good idea, but he couldn't stand by and watch the brute torture the helpless man any longer.

"I said that's enough," Russell said, again. He grabbed the ravenous dog by the collar and jerked him back.

Butch held on, refusing to let go of the arm.

Madness Rising

Pete grew silent. The painful pleas that left his bloody lips fell silent. He laid in the grass like a rag doll with wide eyes looking into the trees above.

Russell tugged and pulled until the cane corso relinquished his hold on the dead man's gnawed limb.

Butch licked around his maw as he huffed through his enlarged nostrils. Max flanked the hulking beast as they sniffed the hunter's motionless corpse.

Damn it.

The last thing Russell wanted was to kill the man. He wasn't a murderer, and regretted having to shoot the hunter.

Perhaps he's still alive, Russell thought as he crouched down next to Pete. He knew better from the dark red splotch on his jacket.

Russell checked Pete's pulse on the side of his neck. His two fingers struggled to find any sign of life.

Butch looked at Russell as Max sniffed at the hunter's head. He yawned, then diverted his gaze out to the dense land of trees that surrounded them.

"And here I thought I had a temper," Russell said, as he rubbed Butch's head. "You're lucky he didn't shoot you."

Johnson's moans loomed in the air.

Russell stood and turned toward Johnson. Butch growled—another warning from the ever-vigilant sentry.

The woods had grown silent, minus Johnson's whimpers. Russell froze. He tilted his head to the side and trained an attentive ear to the wild.

Something had caught the dog's attention, and Russell feared it was armed.

Derek Shupert

CHAPTER EIGHTEEN

RUSSELL

The dogs bared glistening fangs. Fur stood rigid off their spines as growls loomed from their throats. A threat was drawing closer.

Russell skimmed over the tree line near them, but couldn't spot any movement within the dense woods. Still, something was there.

It had to be Tony. No doubt the gunfire signaled trouble to the other hunter. Pete never said how far away he was. Russell figured they probably kept close to each other, and now Pete's friend was coming to see what happened.

The radio on Pete's hip crackled once more. A voice broke through the white noise, but Russell couldn't make out what was being said.

Screw it. It didn't matter. They had to move while they had the chance to escape, sight unseen. Johnson's moaning was growing louder and would signal their position sooner rather than later.

Russell pulled the two-way from Pete's belt. The palm of his hand hammered his leg as he spoke to the growling canines with a stern and forceful tone. "Come on. Let's go, guys."

They lingered for a moment with their gazes fixed at the dense swatch of trees before complying. Max retreated first, galloping after Russell who raced back to Johnson.

"Butch. Come on." Russell said.

Johnson sat on the ground. His face was scrunched in pain as he squinted. He palmed the side of his upper right thigh as best he could with his cuffed hands.

"Someone or something's close by. We need to move," Russell said. "The dogs are on edge. Could be Pete's pal, Tony."

Short, quick breaths escaped the deputy's open mouth as he looked to the trees. Blood pooled between his fingers, discoloring the light-gray trousers he wore.

"It burns," Johnson said. "Feels like someone has a hot poker in my leg."

"I take it you've never been shot before, then, huh?" Russell asked.

Johnson looked to Russell with a scowl, then said, "No, I haven't. It's not something that I had ever planned on happening."

Russell tucked the pistol into the waistband of his jeans as Butch charged up behind him. "Consider it karma for being a dick. Now, let's get you up. We need to get moving."

Johnson grit his teeth as Russell grabbed his hand and pulled him to his feet. He favored the injured leg and limped when he tried to walk. They weren't going to move as fast as Russell wanted.

Max growled.

Butch followed suit.

Madness Rising

They inched forward through the tall grass.

"No. We're leaving," Russell said, ordering the dogs to stand down.

Johnson got on the move as best he could. He grimaced with each step he took. Labored breaths tainted the air–his leg gave from the slightest pressure.

They needed to move faster. The deputy was limping along at a snail's pace.

Russell dug his hand into the front pocket of his jeans, retrieving the keys to the cuffs. "Stop. Give me your wrists."

Johnson stumbled and turned to Russell. His sweaty, flushed face was sprinkled with dirt. He wiped his arm across his brow, then presented his wrists to Russell. "What are you doing?"

"We need to move faster than this," Russell replied. He unlocked the cuffs and slid them off the deputy's wrists. "Give me your arm."

Russell tucked the cuffs and keys into his back pocket as Johnson tossed his arm over his shoulder. The deputy was a fairly big guy, but nothing Russell couldn't handle. He took the brunt of Johnson's weight as they got back on the move.

Trudging through the tall grass, Johnson led them as best he could. He struggled to focus and keep his attention fixed on where they were heading. The terrain remained level with few steep declines or hills for them to traverse. They moved along the forest floor at a slow pace, weaving in and out of trees.

Max raced by the ambling men and took point while Butch covered their six. He moved at a good clip with his nose trained to the ground. The German shepherd didn't stray too far ahead and kept in view of the battered men.

Russell's energy was waning. His overall well-being was declining with every step he took. The withdrawals of not having

159

sufficient alcohol in his system, plus being dehydrated and hungry, was plummeting him closer to a shutdown.

Lugging the injured deputy through the woods only zapped what reserves he had left. Stopping wasn't an option, though. It was life or death now. They'd have to wait to rest until they were in the clear.

The radio on Russell's hip slapped against his leg. An angry, distorted voice shouted through the speaker. Russell picked up a few key words within the white noise, but it wasn't much.

Deadman.

Shot.

Gutted.

That's all he needed to hear. Tony was coming for them, and he wasn't far behind?

Russell peered over Johnson's shoulder. Butch trotted behind them with his nose to the ground. Russell didn't spot Tony stalking them from the dense thickets, but that didn't mean he wasn't there.

A sharp crackle echoed through the trees, followed by a buzzing sound. Russell flinched. His head moved from side to side, searching for the source.

The lone bullet grazed the side of the tree they stumbled past. Chunks of bark were torn from the trunk and fluttered in the air.

Russell ducked his head as Johnson gasped.

"Doesn't look like Tony's as good of a shot as Pete," Russell said, aloud as he stumbled.

It was that, or he was still too far away to get a clean shot at them. Either way, Russell kept moving as fast as they could go. He wanted to keep as much distance between them as he could. Their survival depended on it.

"There." Johnson pointed to an embankment ahead of them. "We get down in there, we might be able to lose him."

Madness Rising

The men lumbered through the vegetation to the edge of the embankment. It wasn't too deep, but enough where they would vanish from Tony's sight.

Johnson removed his arm from around Russell and toed the edge. He dropped down to his backside. A grunt of discomfort fled his lips. He slid down the dirt embankment to the rocky floor.

"Come on, boys," Russell said, as he followed suit.

He slalomed down the grade after Johnson with Max and Butch flanking him on either side.

They hit the bottom near Johnson who was palming his leg. Russell wobbled, lightheaded. He lifted his arms and stabled his equilibrium.

Russell wrapped his arm around the deputy's waist. They hoofed it down the dried-up creek bed. The brittle branches snapped as they stomped through the mushy soil.

Max stopped, then lifted his paw. His nose tested the air as his ears twitched.

Russell couldn't detect any footfalls and wanted to keep going. The more distance they put between Tony and them, the better off they'd be.

They brushed past Max who lowered his head and trotted after them. His tongue hung from the side of his mouth as he continued sniffing the ground.

Butch remained a few paces back, but didn't fall too far behind. He galloped past Russell and Johnson and trotted alongside Max.

The row of trees and bushes that lined the embankment helped conceal their whereabouts. Small gaps within the vegetation only offered brief snippets of what might be lurking above.

The clouds overhead refused to leave, keeping the radiant sun from beating down on the heavily wooded area.

A blast of wind tore through the creek bed. The breeze slammed into Russell's sweaty body, offering a bit of reprieve.

Both canines took off in a dead sprint, leaving Russell and Johnson behind. Russell whistled at the galloping dogs as they made the bend up ahead and vanished from sight.

"I'm going to need to rest a minute." Johnson panted. Each breath was labored.

Russell was beyond spent. His body was running off pure adrenaline and determination, which wouldn't hold up in the long run. "Let's go a bit farther, then we'll stop."

Johnson sighed but didn't counter Russell's suggestion.

The rocky, dry bed became damp. Dirt morphed to soft mud as theirs boots squished through the spongy ground. Water.

The mere thought of having a drink of water pushed Russell on. His arid mouth begged for a drink as his tongue licked across his tacky gums and dried lips.

Dirt morphed to water that grew deeper the farther they trudged through the creek bed. Around the bend, Russell spotted Butch and Max drinking from the stream.

Thank God.

The gurgle of the water filled Russell's ears. The subtle, quaint sound brought a relieved smile to his tired face. He removed his arm from around Johnson's waist, then dropped to his knees.

Russell dipped his cupped hands below the surface. The chilled water ran up his forearms, soaking the ends of his long-sleeved flannel shirt. He brought his hands to his mouth and gulped down the refreshing liquid.

Johnson parroted Russell. He laid on his side and took large gulps from the flowing water. They lingered for a few moments, getting their fill while they could.

Madness Rising

Butch lifted his head from the stream. Water dripped from his damp maw as his tongue licked around the edge. Max followed suit. They looked about the sides of the embankment.

Russell didn't listen for any footfalls or rustling of bushes. The stern, rigid stance from the dogs was more than enough incentive to get him to his feet and back on the move.

Johnson doused his face with water, then ran his fingers through his dingy hair. He flicked his wrists, slinging the water from his hands.

"Come on. We need to keep moving," Russell said.

The few handfuls of water he got wasn't nearly enough to curb the thirst he had, but it would have to do for now.

"Screw it. Just leave me here," Johnson said.

"No can do." Russell grabbed the deputy by the arm and jerked him from the side of the embankment. "I still need you. Now let's move."

Johnson complained like a stubborn kid, but complied just the same.

Russell shouldered his weight as they tromped through the running water.

Butch and Max galloped on either side of them.

Water splashed with every step they took. Their boots sunk below the surface. It was getting deeper the farther they went up stream.

Off to their left was a narrow path that led back up to the forest floor. Russell whistled at the dogs as he veered toward the uneven dirt trail.

Max changed course, then raced up the path with Butch flanking him. The canines disappeared beyond the shrubs and trees, but Russell could hear them milling about.

Johnson lumbered up the dirt incline as best he could while Russell spotted him. A slew of cuss words flowed from his mouth as he trudged past the edge of the embankment.

Russell clawed his way up next to Johnson. Both men wheezed. Butch and Max panted as they stared at the tired men.

They continued on through the forest, shuffling heavy feet through the layers of green leaves that carpeted the ground for a bit longer before Russell spotted a structure in the distance. He squinted his eyes and opened them wide, unsure if his frazzled mind was playing tricks on him.

"I think I see something up ahead," Russell said, while lugging the deputy at his side. "A cabin maybe. Not sure."

Johnson lifted his weary head, and looked in the direction Russell was pointing in. "Yeah, I'm seeing the same thing."

"We can hold up in there for a bit. Give us a chance to catch our breath and lay low," Russell said.

As much as he didn't want to stop, his body, and Johnson's, weren't going to go along. The harder and longer he pushed on without rest, the less good he'd be once they made it to Marcus's place. He had to play it smart, or he'd never make it back to Sarah.

A small make-shift rope bridge hung over the free-flowing stream and provided a way across to the cabin. It looked rickety at best and old. The rope was worn and frayed. Planks of wood were missing at random spots.

Max took the lead and trotted over the bridge first. His claws scraped against each plank. He jumped over the missing ones. The bridge swayed from side to side as he trotted across.

Butch stood at the entrance, then glanced at Russell who wasn't far behind. He toed the edge, but didn't go on.

"What's the matter?" Russell asked as the cane corso stared at him. "Go on. Get across."

Butch huffed, then trekked over the bridge with little effort.

Madness Rising

"Here. You go first," Russell said.

Johnson hobbled across the bridge with him close behind. They stepped over the missing planks and kept going without breaking their stride.

Russell reached for Johnson who waved him off.

"I got it. It's not too much farther."

Russell didn't offer again and moved ahead of the limping deputy. His hand pulled the pistol from his waistband as they closed in on the derelict cabin. He skimmed over the immediate area for any movement.

Trees surrounded the tiny log house along with bushes that lined the side closest to them. The rich greenery climbed the walls of the weathered planks of wood to the ramshackle roof. It didn't look as though anyone was home, but Russell wasn't positive.

Max investigated the front of the cabin while Butch sniffed along the base of the bushes. He trotted along, stopping on a dime, then changing direction. Russell figured the cane corso was looking for a place to relieve himself, even though he could go wherever. It made no sense to Russell, but it didn't have to.

He skimmed over the front of the cabin with the pistol up and at the ready. He couldn't spot any movement through the grime-coated windows.

Max milled about the entrance, sniffing at the front door, then moving down the porch to the far side of the cabin. No warnings came from either dog which set Russell at ease.

Johnson palmed his leg. A flustered look resided on his face as he caught up to Russell. He was still limping and favoring the wound, but he wasn't gripping it as much.

"Anyone in there?" He winced and gritted his teeth.

Russell stepped up onto the porch while trying to pierce the smudged glass of the window to his left. "Don't know for sure, but the dogs aren't growling or barking, which is a good sign."

The boards creaked as he stalked to the front door. The wood was old and showed signs of deterioration. Fragments of the exterior had been chipped away at the bottom.

Johnson limped onto the porch, then made his way to the window off to Russell's right. The deputy craned his neck and stayed to the far side of the window. He pressed his shoulder to the wood and leaned in close.

Russell trained the pistol at the seam of the jamb while grabbing the doorknob with his free hand.

"Looks clear to me," Johnson said, while turning away from the window.

Russell pressed the side of his head to the door and listened. It was silent. Not a single sign of life tickled his ear from inside. He didn't want to be careless, though, and just stroll in with his guard down. Doing so could cost him his life.

CHAPTER NINETEEN

SARAH

The world was an endless nightmare with no end in sight.

Sarah fought to get free of the large, bald man who had taken her from the car. Her legs kicked at the air as she thrashed her head about with reckless abandon. She fought to worm her way free of his hold any way she could. It did little good to better her situation and only served to grow a pounding headache that swelled unchallenged in her head.

The brute huffed and sighed as he lugged her through the building located on the dock. Sarah captured brief snippets of the water and ships out to sea before everything went black.

"Let me go," she said.

The man stopped, then dropped Sarah on her feet. She wobbled in place, swaying back and forth, then from side to side. He bent down and wrapped his thick arms around her waist.

Sarah tried to run away, but the disorientation swelling in her head kept her from escaping his hold.

He slung her over his shoulder with ease and stood up straight.

Sarah was draped over his wide body like a sack of potatoes. Her hair reached for the ground and impeded her vision. It wouldn't have mattered since the building was dim. The only source of light came from the windows high on the sides of the walls near the ceiling.

"Where are you taking me?" Her voice was thick with revulsion. "What do you want with me?"

The brute kept walking. He shoved his free hand into the front pocket of his jeans and removed a flashlight. He thumbed the button on the side, bringing to light the interior of the structure.

Stacks of crates and other boxes acted like walls.

The brute weaved through the never-ending maze of containers.

Sarah kicked her legs, and fought to wiggle free of the man's arm.

Chatter loomed close by. It was low and muffled.

Sarah turned her head from side to side searching for the source of the voices, but only found wooden crates and other large boxes.

The stale smell of cigarette smoke filled the air. It made her nose crinkle and her stomach turn. Blood rushed to her head and compounded her already pounding headache that much more. She was tired of being manhandled, but was powerless to stop it.

Anger turned to fright. Thoughts of the men having free rein over her and Mandy stuck to her brain like glue. It made her feel helpless and alone. If only she had invited Russell over that fateful day when he called to let her know he was going out of town, then perhaps things would be different. Despite his shortcomings and addictions, she'd gladly trade everything to be with him over where she was heading.

A heavy thumping caught her attention. It echoed down the long, dark hallway they were walking through. The sound stopped for a few seconds, then picked up again. An angry, muffled voice barked following each hard rap.

The noise grew louder, more defined, the closer they got. It was definitely a person pounding away at a door or wall.

Sarah thought of Mandy. She was a fireball. Full of grit and spice that didn't always make everything nice. She was a force to be reckoned with when she was done wrong. The old adage rang true; hell hath no fury like a woman scorned, or pissed off for that matter.

"Let me out of here, now," The enraged feminine voice said, at the top of her lungs. "I have friends who are on the Boston Police Force. You asswipes are going to be so sorry!"

Fists continued to hammer the wood, rattling the door.

Brute stopped, then turned toward the ruckus. The flashlight trained at his boots. The darkness swarmed them, with no other light visible except for the dull white beam.

Sarah wiggled her head, trying to flick the strands of her hair away from her face. She glanced down the hall from where they had come from. Two shadowy figures lurched in the darkness. Only their vague outlines could be seen. The red glow of something burning hovered in the air as they hooked a left and vanished beyond the wall.

"Stop that yelling and carrying on, or I'll give you something to scream about," the Irishman said. He kicked the base of the door, then hammered his fist on it with two hard raps.

The shouting ceased, as did the punishment of the door.

Mandy?

The enraged voice on the other side of the door sounded like her. Sarah longed to see a familiar face.

Brute pushed open the door, and stomped inside like a raging bull. He huffed and sighed. Each breath exhaled was filled with annoyance.

Shoes shuffled along the floor away from the menacing man. Then silence. He slung Sarah forward, dropping her on her feet. She stood in front of the towering man who was cast in partial shadows.

A hint of light gleamed over the cheerless white walls. Perhaps from a lantern of some sort. Thick darkness loomed from the hallway with little to no hint of sunlight.

Brute grabbed Sarah's arm and spun her around. The sudden movement made her wobble and sway.

In the corner of the room was the woman who had been screaming. She kept her distance from the agitated man as she looked their way. Her arms were folded across her chest as she paced about the corner. It looked like Mandy, but Sarah couldn't be sure.

Brute pulled a knife from his pants, and cut the zip tie from Sarah's wrists, freeing her. Her skin stung from where the plastic had sliced into flesh. The bones of her wrists were sore to the touch.

"I don't want to hear anymore screaming or carrying on. Am I understood?" Brute pointed the tip of his blade at the woman.

She nodded.

Brute retreated back through the open doorway, and slammed the door shut.

Sarah moved her arms from behind her back. The motion hurt and made her pause. Her muscles were stiff and rigid. The joints ached and throbbed. She inspected her wrists and forearms which were painted with strokes of red. A mixture of dried and tacky blood clung to her skin.

Sarah grimaced as she touched the injured spots while looking at the woman. "Mandy, is that you?"

Madness Rising

"Sarah?" The woman stepped away from the wall and crept closer to her. The light from the lantern on the desk to her left washed over her face, revealing her best friend's smeared makeup. She offered a warm smile, followed by tears that rushed from both eyes.

"Oh, Sarah." Mandy rushed toward Sarah who embraced her with open arms. They held each other close while weeping and crying tears of joy. Sarah wished it was under better circumstances, but she'd take it none-the-less.

"I am so happy to see you," Sarah said, whimpering. "I've been trying to get to you for the past few days. So much has happened. I tried to call, but the phones stopped working. I haven't been able to reach anyone. Not even Russell, so I don't know if he is even ok or not."

Mandy hugged her neck a few seconds longer before backing away. She dipped her chin and wiped away the tears from her eyes. "Likewise. I was waiting for you at Copley Place, wondering where the hell you were. I tried to call you. I figured you were probably trying to back out on me or something like that. You know how you are. When I tried to call you, I got the same thing. No cell service. Then the power crashed, and well, that's when everything went to hell."

Sarah grabbed Mandy's chin, then tilted her face to the side. It was hard to tell if she had any bruises or cuts on her face from the shadows and smeared makeup. "Are you ok? Aside from looking like a rock band groupie, I don't see any bruises or what not."

Mandy sneered, then knocked her hand away. "Funny. I haven't seen my face since being brought here. The bathroom over there has a toilet and sink, but the water pressure is abysmal with the power being out. No mirror either. I'd be willing to bet, though, that I look a lot better than you."

The side of Sarah's face still stung from the backhand she received from Man-bun. She probed the puffy skin with her fingers. A shot of pain made Sarah wince, then move her hand away.

"Yeah. Some guy in a man-bun was waiting in your apartment when me and David arrived. It went downhill from there."

Mandy's face lit up hearing David's name, but soon evaporated after realizing that Sarah was alone. Her wide, hopeful eyes drooped as her body deflated. "Is he ok?"

Sarah wasn't sure how to respond or if she wanted to. His death clung to her back like a bad stench. She felt responsible for what had happened to him. She looked away. "He's... It's..."

Tears rolled from Sarah's eyes. The loss of her good friend hurt her soul and added to the overabundance of pain that had already punished her so much.

"Oh, no," Mandy gasped. Her hand covered her mouth as she stared at Sarah. "What happened to him?"

"Man-bun did something with him. I'm not sure what, though." Sarah fought to control her emotions. Her fingers pressed to her nose as she sniffled. The overwhelming wave of guilt was cresting and ready to crash into her. "It's all my fault."

Mandy placed her hand on Sarah's shoulder. A look of sadness rested on her face. "Don't be so hard on yourself. Whatever happened is not your fault. It's those BASTARDS OUT THERE!" Her voice boomed like thunder in the enclosed space. The revulsion for the vile men was unmistakable. Despite having been threatened by the brute, Mandy continued her tongue lashing.

Sarah gathered herself and focused her thoughts away from David as Mandy pushed past her.

"Where are you going?" Sarah asked.

Mandy rushed the entrance. Her fingers balled into tight fists. She hammered the door and kicked the scuffed wood at the bottom. "Hey, assholes! You're so going to pay for everything you've done. Mark my words, I'm going to make sure each of you hangs for this."

The door rattled from each hard blow Mandy dealt. She wasn't thinking straight. Their captors had warned her to keep it down, and not make any more noise, or else.

"Hey, maybe you should ease up," Sarah urged. "That guy from earlier seemed pretty pissed with you. The last thing we need to do is-"

The door opened. A dark mass stood in the black hallway. The light from their room outlined his wide frame.

Mandy retreated with her fist still in the air.

The man stormed inside the room and grabbed her arm. What Sarah could see of his face was twisted into a scowl. His nostrils flared. "I thought I told you to stop that."

"Let me go, you neanderthal." Mandy jerked her arm, trying to free herself of the brute's hold.

Sarah reached toward them. "Let her go and I'll make sure she doesn't-"

The disgruntled hulk smacked Mandy across the face. Mandy's head snapped to the side as her body went limp. She crumpled to the floor.

Sarah rushed to her aid. The brute held his arm in the air, stopping Sarah dead in her tracks. He pointed at the wafer-thin cot that was pushed against the wall. "Sit down and shut up. I better not hear so much as a peep out of you."

"What are you going to do with my friend?" Sarah asked as she stood her ground. "Who are you people, and what the hell do you want with us?"

The brute stared at Sarah without blinking. His lips pursed as the muscles in his arms twitched and flexed through his shirt. "Just shut up."

He bent down and peeled Mandy off the floor. Her head bobbled about as her legs struggled to hold her up. She looked like a marionette doll that was fixed with strings.

"Please, sir. I'll keep quiet," Sarah said.

Brute turned toward the open doorway and dragged Mandy to the dark hallway. She stumbled over her feet as she glanced back over her shoulder. Muttered words fled her feeble lips as she lifted her arm in protest.

Sarah inched forward and reached out to her best friend. The brute skirted the jamb with Mandy in tow. Her fingers latched onto the frame for only a second as fearful eyes looked to Sarah.

Mandy vanished into the blackness as a brief scream fled her lips. A ghastly gray figure loomed beyond the room, then slammed the door shut, sealing Sarah inside.

CHAPTER TWENTY

RUSSELL

The ramshackle cabin was a safe haven among the densely populated woods.

That was the best way to describe the eerie place they had stumbled upon. It was shelter, and kept them hidden from the hunter tracking them. That, in and of itself, made it more appealing than anything the great outdoors had to offer.

"Well, it's not the Hilton or Club Med. That's for sure," Johnson said, while looking over the drab interior with a disgusted expression. "But I guess beggars can't be choosers, huh?"

The cabin was less than appealing. The floor felt weak under Russell's feet. The scuffed boards sagged with each step he took.

Russell's nose crinkled as he caught a whiff of something foul. Perhaps feces from an animal. He glanced at the floor, but couldn't spot any droppings within the layers of dust that had collected. Between that and the stale smell, it made for an unpleasant experience.

A few wooden rocking chairs and a cot, with a less than desirable mattress that was discolored and torn, rounded out the place.

"I wouldn't get too comfortable," Russell said, from the make-shift kitchen that was nestled in the back corner of the tiny cabin. "We're not going to be here that long. We catch our breath, and lay low until it's safe. I want to be back on the move in a bit."

Johnson rolled his eyes while limping around the cabin. "You don't have to ask me twice. I think I'd rather take my chances out there than stay in here." A look of disgust washed over his dingy, sweaty face. His hand ran along the top of one of the wooden rocking chairs that was draped in cobwebs.

The sticky silk bound to his fingers as he pulled it away. He didn't care for the accommodations, that much was obvious. Still, the cabin was a means to an end, and for now, it was serving its purpose.

"Look at that. We at least have a sunroof," Johnson said, while pointing to the few large holes in the ceiling.

Beams of light funneled through busted portions of the roof, allowing what bit of radiance the trees allowed inside.

"Why don't you sit, and take some pressure off that leg. I'll see if maybe there's anything of use in these cabinets we can dress it with," Russell said. "That might be a long shot, but we'll see."

Johnson limped around the front of the chair. He grumbled while taking a seat. His hand pressed to the side of his leg as he leaned back.

Max and Butch sniffed around the cabin for a bit before hopping up onto the bed. The springs squeaked as they sat down. Both panted, tongues dangling from their maws. They appeared to be happy with just getting a moment's rest, and didn't seem to mind the filth of the cabin. Russell felt much the same.

Russell turned toward the rickety cabinetry in the corner of the cabin. There were two sets of upper and lower cupboards. The doors sat crooked with some hanging from their hinges. A piece of plywood acted as a makeshift countertop. The rigid wood surface was stained red, which had seeped into the grain. Rusted pots and pans were scattered along the top of the counter. Their bottoms and sides were blackened.

"Doesn't look like anyone's been here for some time," Russell said, as he skimmed over everything. "I'm kind of glad. I'm getting a real backwoods hillbilly horror vibe here."

Off to the side of the cabinets was a wood burning heater. The black, cast iron firebox looked to be in relatively good shape. One of the few items in the cabin that were.

"Well, I'd be lying if I said there weren't. There are some crazy-ass people in these hills that do some pretty disgusting things. I'll spare you the details."

"I appreciate that," Russell replied.

Johnson tore the side of his trousers to get a better look at the wound. His leg rotated to the side far enough for him to inspect the damage. "Looks like the bullet caught the outside of my leg. I think it went straight through, though."

Russell sifted through the cabinets, opening each door cautiously. He wasn't a fan of rodents and figured the cabin would house the dreadful vermin.

"So, you're not going to lose the leg, then?" he asked, jabbing the deputy with his snide comment.

"No, and that's the least of my worries, no thanks to you." Johnson shot back.

"Hey, we could've stayed on the highway, but because of you, we're now knee-deep in backwoods country, so I don't want to hear it," Russell said.

The cabinets were bare of anything of use. He found nothing more than some empty glass jars and more animal droppings. Perhaps from mice or rats. Russell didn't know which one and it didn't matter. Either way, the thought made him shudder.

Russell slammed the door, then stooped down. The foul smell grew as he reached for the cabinet in front of him. He opened it up and found a large rat lying dead on its side. His face contorted as he palmed his mouth and nose. The smell and sight of the decaying rodent did enough to curb his famished stomach.

He continued checking the remaining cupboards. They had nothing of use within the mess of cobwebs except for one. Nestled in the back of the dark cabinet, Russell spied a bottle of some sort. He reached to the wall and grabbed the top.

"Find anything of use?" Johnson asked from his chair.

"A dead rat. Hungry?"

Johnson gagged.

Russell smirked as he pulled the bottle free of the cabinet. His eyes lit up like a kid at Christmas. Excitement swelled inside of him.

The brown tinted liquor sloshed about in the dirty bottle. Russell swiped his thumb across the front, revealing a whiskey maker from years past.

"I did find this. Care for a drink?" Russell turned toward Johnson and shook the never opened bottle. "Might help with any pain."

"A rat and whiskey. We're saved," Johnson said, in a condescending tone. "I think I'll pass. Looking at everything else in here and smelling that dead rodent, the only thing that sounds good is more water."

Russell shrugged. "Suit yourself."

Johnson pointed at the bottle, then said, "How do you even know it's still good. From the layer of dust and who knows what else, it could've been down there for years. Decades."

"Whiskey doesn't really go bad if the seal hasn't broken," Russell said. "If it has been, then it will slowly weaken over time and lose its flavor, but that's about it."

"I guess you'd know all about that, huh, Cage?" Johnson asked.

The disparaging remark was not lost on Russell, but he didn't care. Johnson had no place to judge him.

Staring at the bottle, Russell caught a glimpse of something tucked under the bed. It was hard to tell what it was. He set the aged whiskey on the floor and bent over. The side of his face kissed the dirt as he reached into the depths under the steel frame of the cot. He grabbed a handful of what felt like a pack or something and pulled it out.

"Did you find more whiskey?" Johnson quipped.

Russell gave him the middle finger. A thick layer coated the outside of the dark green and brown rucksack. Russell unzipped the pack and opened it up.

The interior was stuffed with an array of items. Rope, batteries, flashlight, a canteen, and first aid kit.

"Here," Russell said, while throwing the first aid kit at Johnson.

"Whoa." Johnson fumbled the kit in his hands.

Russell pulled the canteen out of the pack and stood up. He grabbed the bottle from the floor and turned toward the open door. "I'm going to go down to the stream and fill this up. Get that leg dressed however you need and be ready to move."

Johnson popped the top to the kit. It was stocked with an assortment of bandages, gauze, and other medical items. "Enjoy that whiskey, Cage."

Asshole.

"Just hurry it up." Russell tromped to the open doorway. Max fell in line behind him as did Butch. He stopped, then turned toward the dogs. "Butch, you stay and watch after him, all right?"

Butch looked up to Russell blankly. He peered back to Johnson who was sifting through the contents of the medical kit.

Max skirted around Russell and bolted from the cabin.

Russell nodded at Butch who stood in the middle of the cabin. The cane corso plopped down on his haunches, and obeyed Russell's command.

"Good boy."

The door closed behind Russell. He exhaled a deep breath of frustration. Johnson had a way of crawling under his skin with the slightest comment or gesture. Perhaps it was the fact that Russell knew he had a problem and was losing the battle in resisting the temptation. At that moment, with all things consider, it didn't seem as big of an issue. Maybe it would help cure what ailed him.

Russell secured the brown leather strap attached to the canteen across his body. He moved across the porch to the ground where Max was sniffing. His eyes couldn't help but fix on the bottle of whiskey. The brown tinted liquor filled his gaze as his mouth watered on its own. Just looking at the bottle made him anxious with excitement. His tongue slid over his lips as he swallowed the lump in his throat.

Temptation was a bitch. One that Russell was too weak to battle in his current state. The amount of stress racking him through and through was enough to make anyone want a drink.

Screw it.

Madness Rising

Russell broke the seal and twisted the cap free of the bottle. The rich scent of the whiskey escaped the opening and filled his nose. He took a hefty swig of the potent liquor. His taste buds danced and rejoiced from the sweet, familiar taste splashing over his tongue and racing to his stomach.

He removed the bottle from his lips, savoring the flavor of the spirit that helped ease his mind and steady his nerves. Johnson was right about one thing. Going cold turkey would only end in disaster, and there were plenty of disasters happening all around him already.

For now, Russell would need to do whatever was necessary to not fall apart, physically or emotionally. When the time was right, and he was back with Sarah, then he'd tackle his demons. Until then, he needed their help and welcomed them inside.

Russell took another swig from the bottle before securing the cap back on. Some restraint had to be shown. If he kept drinking, he'd polish it off in no time and that simply wouldn't do. It was a means to an end, and he needed to stretch it out for as long as he could.

Max milled about the open plot of grassy land before the bridge. His tail danced and swayed from side to side. His nose trained to the ground as if he was hot on a scent.

The bottle of whiskey dangled between Russell's fingers as he tracked him down. A warm, soothing sensation flooded his body as he skimmed over the woods and listened for any hints of the hunter or other threats. It was quiet, aside from the chirping of birds and the wind rustling the trees around them.

"What do you think, boy. Are you missing Cathy?" Russell asked as he kneaded the crown of the German shepherd's head.

Max tilted his head back and glanced at Russell with his big, soulful eyes. His ears perked from hearing Cathy's name, and his tongue flicked at Russell's hand.

"Yeah. Shouldn't be too much longer, bud." Russell patted his side, then strolled to the edge of the drop off near the bridge. The land seemed higher where he stood than where they were before. There was no gradual slope, but more of a straight drop to the bottom.

Max stood at his side and toed the edge while glancing at the glistening stream.

Russell evaluated his options. Trudging back to the spot where they climbed out would take more time. He wanted to stay close, get the water, and move on. Sitting down and getting too comfortable felt like a death sentence, as he feared his body wouldn't want to get back up.

The trees and bushes that lined the creek to his right hindered his view. There had to be an accessible way to the stream from where the cabin was. Why else would they have built it so close if there wasn't?

Russell stepped out onto the bridge and craned his neck. His hands wrapped around the tattered rope as he leaned forward. The creek slithered through the land, then cut sharply to the right with no visible way down to the water.

"What do you think?" Russell asked Max.

The German shepherd groaned, then sat on his haunches. He lifted his hind leg and tended to an itch that bit at his private area.

"Yeah. My thoughts exactly."

On the far side of the creek, near the bend, Russell noticed a patch of dirt and rocks near the water. From where he stood, it looked wide enough for him to stand on and gather some water.

"Come on, Max. I think I found our way down."

Madness Rising

Russell trekked across the bridge to the other side with Max in tow. It swayed, but the ropes held. In the back of his mind, the hunter loomed as a wild card still in play. Russell hoped they had done a good enough job giving him the slip, but it was unclear if they had. They'd have to remain vigilant.

Max ran past Russell as they hit dirt on the far side. He rummaged through the tall grass and bushes, then darted past Russell.

The energizer bunny spawned inside Russell's head as he watched Max zip about the wooded area. The German shepherd was full of energy that never waned. If Russell could syphon just a smidge of the rambunctious dog's energy, it would do him a world of good.

Russell walked the side of the creek while skimming over the dense woods. His free hand rested on the grip of the pistol as his other clutched the bottle.

The sun took refuge behind the bloated clouds that seemed to follow no matter where they went. A hint of rain lingered in the air. A dark gloom blanketed the area, casting portions of the woods in an eerie gray hue.

The mountain lion that almost stole his life after they first crashed came to mind. Its tawny fur was ingrained inside his mind as well as the sharp claws and fangs. He could still feel the pressure from the cat's powerful jaws on his forearm.

Russell shook the thought from his head and focused on the task at hand as he made the bend. He skirted past a tree and eyed the portion of the creek bed he'd spotted from the bridge.

Max trotted to his side.

A flash of brown zipped down the tree about ten feet away. A low growl loomed from Max's throat, followed by a bark. His body tensed as his ears stood on end. He honed in on the small mammal and inched forward.

"Max, stay. It's just a-" The canine took off after the squirrel in a dead sprint. He vanished into the grass, then the bushes. "Max. Get back here, now!"

The stern warning did little good. The German shepherd was hot on the trail of the squirrel, leaving Russell alone. He didn't have time to track him down, and he'd probably lose interest and be back before Russell got up top.

Russell dropped the whiskey next to the base of the tree he stood by as he skimmed over the slope. He gave one final look to the area close by for an easier way down, but couldn't find one. He contemplated waiting on the water, but wasn't sure which way they were heading, or if Johnson needed any to dress his wound. Lugging the deputy any farther didn't appeal to Russell either.

All right, let's get this done.

Russell toed the edge and leaned forward. Footfalls tingled his ears. The fine hairs on the back of his neck stood on end. He pulled the pistol from his waistband and spun around on the heels of his boots to find Tony rushing headlong at him.

The hunter bulldozed through the grass. He tugged at the trigger, but the rifle didn't respond. He flipped it around, then lifted it in the air. The hunter sneered and wielded the rifle like a baseball bat.

Russell squeezed the trigger.

Tony swung the rifle at Russell's arm as fire spat from the barrel. The bullet went wide, grazing Tony's jacket. The sidearm dropped from Russell's hand.

"You're a dead man, pal," Tony said. The hunter flipped the rifle about as Russell cradled his forearm. He slammed the buttstock into Russell's stomach.

Madness Rising

Russell doubled over, then dropped to his knees. He struggled to breathe as pain lanced up his arm.

"Who are you, and why did you kill my friend?" Tony asked as he trained the rifle at Russell's head. "I saw the hole in Pete's chest. You're no hunter. That's apparent from the way you're dressed. Plus, you're carrying a police-issued firearm."

Russell's gaze flitted to Tony who had him dead to rights. A simple pull of the trigger and fragments of his head would paint the grass and dirt. He fought to catch his breath.

Tony leaned forward and pressed the end of the barrel to Russell's forehead. "Last time I'm going to ask. Who are you and why-"

The grass thrashed behind Tony, pulling his attention away from Russell. Max charged from the thick blades with his maw open.

Russell knocked the barrel of the rifle away from his head as the hunter tugged on the trigger again.

The rifle discharged.

A flash of fire breathed from the barrel.

The thunderous explosion battered his ears as he lunged forward, spearing Tony in the stomach.

Both men hit the ground hard.

Russell mounted the hunter, then grabbed the rifle with both hands. Tony gnashed his teeth as his body wiggled under Russell's weight.

Max snapped at Tony's arm and head. Tony tried to scoot away.

"You made a big mistake here," he said, through his clenched jaw. "You have no idea who you're dealing... aah!"

Max grabbed a chunk of Tony's bicep and shook his head while tugging.

Tony jerked his arm free of Max's mouth, ripping the sleeve of his coat on the ravenous dog's fangs. He lifted his hips into the air, then turned away from Max. Momentum threw Russell from the hunter's waist to the grass. He rolled across the ground and over his pistol.

A sharp yelp rang out which was dulled by the ringing in Russell's left ear. He scooped up the pistol and got to his knees just as Tony brought his rifle to bear.

"Don't do it, pal," Russell said, warning the hunter. The barrel lined up with Tony's torso. "I don't want to kill you, but I will if I have to."

Tony's brow furrowed. His face twisted angrily as he glared at Russell. He hesitated for a moment with the rifle shouldered and the barrel trained just to the side of Russell's chest.

"You made a huge mistake here today. You're nothing more than a dead man walking," Tony said.

Russell didn't flinch from the idle threat, but dreaded what he feared was coming next. Tony showed no signs of yielding. He kept his rifle shouldered. The barrel of Russell's pistol stayed fixed at the hunter. Neither man was willing to give up. Someone was going to die.

Tony wrenched the rifle up.

Russell squeezed the trigger.

A single round fired from his pistol.

The lone bullet struck the hunter in the upper right shoulder.

Tony yelled out in pain as he fell back onto the ground. The rifle fell from his hands to the grass. He palmed his shoulder.

Max stalked the man.

"No. Leave him be," Russell said.

The German shepherd looked to Russell, then back to Tony while growling.

Madness Rising

Russell sprang into action. The pistol trembled in his hand as he trained the weapon at Tony. He grabbed the hunter's rifle and tossed it to the creek bed.

The radio on his hip crackled with more stressed voices speaking through the white noise. It was unclear of their position, but waiting around any longer wasn't an option. They had to keep moving.

"When the boss man catches up to you, he's going to skin you alive," Tony said. "You better kill me now because if you don't, I'm-"

Russell slammed the pistol into the side of Tony's head, stopping his rambling and idle threats.

Max sniffed his body, and kept watch for any sudden movements.

Russell ripped the radio from Tony's belt, then tossed it to the creek with the rifle. He hated the fact that he was forced to shoot another man, but doing so had saved Russell's life.

A dense thumping stalked Russell from behind. He spun around, and took aim at whatever was charging his way.

Butch was closing in fast. The cane corso had his head lowered and eyes fixed on Tony's motionless body.

"Hey. You all right?" Johnson asked from across the creek, parts of his body concealed by the bushes and trees that rimmed the edge.

Russell lowered the pistol and exhaled as Butch licked at his face. "Yeah. I'm good, but we need to move. More might be coming."

Derek Shupert

CHAPTER TWENTY-ONE

SARAH

The silence was deafening and did little to stay Sarah's nerves. Every thought she had repressed came spilling out all at once—a wave of painful emotions she couldn't contain any longer.

Sarah sat on the razor thin mattress with her back against the wall. A long, lost look filled her shiny eyes as she stared off into space. Streams of hopeless tears raced down her warm, flushed cheeks. She didn't want to die in that building, or have something more sinister happen to her or Mandy.

The lantern on the beaten desk across from her flickered. It acted as though it could go at any minute, and cast her into utter darkness. That would be icing on the cake.

The back of Sarah's head gently rapped against the wall as she tried to remain strong and figure out what her next move was going to be. She had no real weapons of any kind.

Her Glock was taken by Man-bun in Mandy's apartment, and her purse was M.I.A. She couldn't remember where she last had it, but it didn't matter much now.

The back of her hand wiped away the tears from both eyes as she scooted off the cot. The springs creaked and popped as Sarah slid toward the edge. Her shoes pressed to the floor. Both arms rested on the soft parts of her knees.

A heavy sigh fled her lips. She didn't know what to do with herself to keep her mind occupied. Despite how hard she tried, she couldn't focus on her current situation.

Sarah cursed Mandy under her breath while picking at the ends of her dirty fingernails. Why couldn't she just be quiet, and follow the rules?

That was rich considering what Sarah had done in Mandy's apartment, and how it got David killed. It was a painful lesson in when to shut up.

Russell squeezed his way into the front of her mind, edging Mandy out. He was always there. Sarah longed to see him again. To reconnect and try to work things out.

The way she acted toward him, distant and like she didn't care, was just her way of coping with the muddled mess. Deep down, where no one could see, Sarah wanted him back in her life. Given her current predicament, though, and Russell missing God knew where, any sort of reconciliation could be too little, too late.

Chatter from beyond the door grabbed Sarah's attention. The silence allowed voices to carry through the walls of her room. She couldn't make out what was being said, or how many people there were.

Madness Rising

Sarah stood from the cot and stared at the door. The lantern flickered, then dimmed some more. The candle's glow lessened, and cast the room further into darkness. Shadows slithered along the walls like demons. An eerie feeling made Sarah clutch her jacket and pull it tighter.

The voices beyond the room grew louder. It sounded as though they were on the other side of the far wall roaming the hall. Her heart thumped harder. The thought of the vile men coming back made her skin crawl. She had no plans of antagonizing them, but she wasn't opposed to defending herself if it came to that.

The desk. It had to have something of use in the drawers. A pencil, pen, or something of the sort she could use as a stabbing weapon. Anything would do.

Sarah rushed to the desk and sifted through the drawers. Time was of the essence not only because of her abductors, but because the lantern's dull glow was waning. Soon, it would be out.

The shadows clinging over the desk made it difficult to see. Sarah grabbed the lantern and pulled it closer. She stooped down and squinted as her fingers rummaged through the array of office supplies that were knocked about the steel drawer.

She slammed the middle door shut, then moved to the one to the right. The noise of metal on metal made her cringe, then freeze. Sarah expected heavy footsteps to tromp her way, but none came.

The drawer was mostly empty with only a few paper clips, and Post-it notes inside. Sarah closed the desk drawer and moved to the next. Her hands trembled with fright and anxiety. She muttered to herself to hurry up, and focus on what she was doing.

The lantern's gleam faded to darkness, and the room went to black. Sarah reached for the light and grabbed the handle on top of the device.

191

"Come on, come on," she said, smacking her palm against the base.

A spark of life breathed from the bulb. Sarah rejoiced with a grin. Light grew from the interior of the clear plastic casing and pushed the darkness back.

She had to move fast. She caught a lucky break and might not be as lucky next time.

One drawer left to check. She jerked it open. The few contents inside knocked about the steel. The brilliance from the lantern waned as she held it a scant inch away from the shallow drawer.

The doorknob to the room twisted as voices beyond the door raised an octave. It sounded heated.

Oh no.

Sarah was out of time. Her pulse spiked as she glanced to the door, then back to the desk.

The tips of her fingers searched the interior as if her life depended on it. Sarah reached to the back of the drawer and discovered a long, slender object. Her finger felt around the flat edge. She couldn't see what it was, but she pulled it out just the same.

Sarah held the knife-like object up to the lantern. A letter opener. She probed the tip with her finger. It was blunt and dull. With enough pressure, though, she might be able to pierce the skin.

The door rattled inside the jamb, then popped open.

"You just worry about yourself and less about what I'm doing," an angry voice said. The door stopped moving. Light from the hall bled into the room. Sarah closed the desk drawer and scurried back to the bed. "You don't get paid to think or have an opinion. Now follow orders. No one asked you, so shut it, all right?"

Madness Rising

Sarah sat on the edge of the cot as the door opened farther. Both of her hands were clasped together between her legs as a smaller, pudgy man stomped into the room.

He huffed and puffed, then shook his head. His cohort loomed from the hallway, but didn't venture inside. He trained the light at the man's back which outlined his shadowy, round silhouette.

The man stood in the middle of the room, staring at Sarah who remained silent and still. His ominous presence made her feel uneasy, causing her to adjust her backside on the bed. Sarah couldn't see his eyes from the partial shadow that covered his face. Only his mouth was visible. A coy smirk formed as his tongue rimmed the edge of his lips. Nestled in the waistband of his jeans, Sarah thought she spotted the outline of a pistol, but couldn't be sure.

Sarah diverted her gaze to the floor, then back to him. He kept his attention fixed in her direction, then cocked his head to the side as if to look her over.

"So, this is our newest catch, huh?" the man said, with a sinister tone. He lifted his arm and motioned for the other man to come closer. "Bring me the light, Martin."

"Um, you know the boss told us to keep out of here, Sonny," Martin replied. "He was quite clear on that point. We're not allowed to come in here at all because of what you did last time."

Sonny sighed, then rubbed his hand over his face. "Yeah, well that was an accident. Just get your ass in here, and bring me the flashlight. I'm not going to ask you again."

Martin hesitated, then looked down either side of the hallway. He inched his way toward the entrance of the room while scanning over the hall.

Sarah gulped, but remained silent. Her gaze switched between Sonny and Martin. The letter opener stayed clutched between her palms and out of sight of the fiendish men.

"Today, Martin," Sonny said, while snapping his fingers.

The rail-thin submissive man flanked the overbearing meat sack. He placed the flashlight in his hand, then quickly back-peddled to the open doorway.

Sarah caught a brief glimpse of a pistol in his jeans. Both men were armed which didn't bode well for her.

Sonny shined the light on Sarah's face. She squinted, then turned away. "She's just as scrumptious as her friend. I'd say this is another good catch. What do you think, newbie? She's pretty hot, huh?"

Martin lingered by the door. He peered out into the darkness, but didn't respond. He seemed more worried about getting caught than about what Sonny was doing.

"I guess so, yeah," Martin said, in a low whisper that was barely audible. Trepidation tainted his voice. "Can we please get out of here before Philip comes back? He's the only one the boss wants in here messing with the girls."

Sonny snickered as he eyed Sarah. "These aren't girls, Martin. They're women. Every single inch is full grown, my friend. Just look at her."

Sarah concealed the letter opener in one hand while raising the other to block the light. The hint of the man's intention was clear as day. The thought of his hands touching her skin made her shudder.

Sitting on the cot, Sarah held her breath as she struggled to keep her fear from spilling out. She pressed her lips together to keep from blurting out a slew of obscenities she feared would only antagonize the deviant.

Madness Rising

"Grab that door, will ya?" Sonny asked. "I just want to get a sneak peek at what goodies our lady friend has to offer."

"Christ. Are you kidding me right now?" Martin hissed. "I'm getting out of here while I can. If you want to stay and get a slug to the head when Philip comes back, that's on you, but I'm not dying from perving on some chick."

Sonny kept his gaze fixed on Sarah as he walked toward her. He reached out to grab her arm, then said, "Just get the damn door. I'll tell Philip you were in here with me if you don't. Who do you think they'll—"

Sarah sprung from the cot, wielding the letter opener like a dagger. She lifted her arm into the air and charged the pudgy swine. Her brow furrowed as she breathed heavily through her nose.

Sonny stumbled backward, his eyes widening from the sudden movement. Nonsense fled his lips as Sarah stabbed him in the side of the neck.

"Aah! Get her off me!" He cried out in pain.

The blunt end punctured the skin.

Blood poured from the narrow slit.

The fat bastard tripped over his feet, and fell to the floor. He groaned in agony and pleaded for Martin to come help.

Sarah mounted his waist.

"I'll go get help," Martin stuttered from the doorway.

The plump guard swatted at Sarah, trying to get her off him.

She knocked his arms out of the way and stabbed him two more times in the neck. Anger filled her soul and spilled out in a swarm of violence that rained down upon the sorry excuse for a human. That would be the closest he would get to having her give him a cheap thrill.

Sonny gurgled on his own blood. His arms swung wildly in the air. He caught a lucky shot, striking Sarah in the face. The blow knocked her off his waist.

The letter opener popped from Sarah's fist as she hit the floor. She searched the floor for the opener, but couldn't find it within the murk.

Sonny tried to speak, but his words came out as nothing more than a garbled mess. Blood erupted from his mouth like hot lava. His hand palmed the multiple stab wounds, but it did little good in staying the flow of blood.

Sarah crawled toward him and reached over his twitching legs. The flashlight sat on the floor with the beam trained at his head. She scooped it up and leaned back.

The light washed over his stomach, and the piece he had tucked in his waistband. Sarah pulled the handgun from his jeans, then stood up. She trained the light at the weapon and caught sight of the red taint that stained her palm.

Both hands were wet with blood, but she didn't care. The opportunity to escape was upon her, and she couldn't let it pass. Martin had vanished from his post, giving Sarah a straight shot to the hallway.

Sonny writhed on the floor as Sarah bolted for the hall. She hoped he suffered a slow, painful death before passing.

Sarah stopped at the open doorway with her arm pressed to the jamb. The pistol trembled in her hand as she panted. A swarm of adrenaline and fright surged through her body as she peered down the hallway.

The flashlight beam sliced through the ether before fading away. It didn't pick up any inbound men charging her way. Sarah stepped to the other side of the entryway with the pistol up and at the ready.

Madness Rising

She craned her neck and skimmed over the vacant corridor. The faint hint of light spilled through the distance, but did little in offering any insight as to what waited for her. Loud, angry shouting caught her attention, followed by multiple footfalls coming her way.

Sarah dipped out into the hall, then scurried down the dark hallway in the opposite direction. The light trained ahead of her as she kept the pistol up. She peered back over her shoulder as the hastened footfalls grew louder.

"We need to find her," a voice said. "We can't lose her."

The pounding of her feet against the floor echoed through the hall. Each hard step signaled her position and made her cringe.

Sarah was lost on where to go. The blinding darkness seemed endless and hid any threats that loomed ahead of her. The flashlight waved like a magical wand in her hand—a powerful weapon at her disposal.

She had to track down Mandy. Leaving her behind wasn't an option, but finding where they were keeping her was easier said than done.

The men were closing in fast. Their footfalls drew closer. The gleam from her light acted like a beacon for them to follow. Sarah couldn't turn it off, though. It was too dark, and she wouldn't be able to see where she was going.

A junction was up ahead. The hall split off to the left with a wall of darkness before her. She saw no hints of lights and didn't hear voices.

Sarah slowed just enough to skirt the blind corner. She peered over her shoulder to the hall while running at full tilt. A few long strides were all she was afforded before running into a black clad figured that felt like a brick wall.

The impact knocked her hard to the floor. The air ripped from her lungs. Both the flashlight and pistol fell from her hands as she struggled to gather herself.

A large man hovered over Sarah. The beam from the flashlight shone on his thick-soled boots. The pistol was within her reach. She reached for the piece, but the man kicked it away. He grabbed a handful of her clothing and jerked her off the floor.

"The boss wants to have a word with you."

CHAPTER TWENTY-TWO

SARAH

The brute slammed Sarah down into a chair. The metal legs scraped across the floor. Sarah's head wobbled and ached.

Natural light shone through the windows and gave her a visual of the warehouse. Stacks of crates and boxes littered the space. A number of armed men stood around with automatic rifles clutched in their hands. There were five that Sarah counted, including Martin. Guess today was his lucky day since he was still breathing.

Mandy sat in a chair across from her. A gag had been placed in her mouth. Muffled screams loomed from the cloth as she leaned forward in the chair.

"I tell you what. I don't think I've ever come across two females who have given me more trouble than you and your friend there," an irritated Irish voice said, from behind Sarah. Footfalls traced behind her and drew closer. Sarah turned her head to either side, trying to lay eyes on the man, but couldn't. "Most are generally too scared to even look at my men. But not you two. Old Sonny found out what sort of a handful you really are, did he?"

He stalked her from behind, then leaned in close to sniff her hair. His fingers ran through the matted strands as he walked around her.

Sarah jerked her head away from his touch while looking in his direction. A scowl formed on her face as she glared at the well-groomed man. "Who are you, and what do you want with me and my friend?"

The tall, stout man walked a bit farther, then turned to face Sarah. Both palms ran over his slicked back hair. He had no facial hair and looked clean and well kept.

"The name is Kinnerk. Samuel Kinnerk to be more precise."

Sarah tensed. Her fingers clawed the tops of her thighs as the blood drained from her face. She glanced around at the armed goons flanking Samuel and noticed two of them who had been after her and Rick. Both looked battered and beaten with black eyes and busted lips. They must have killed Rick, but not before he throttled them. He was yet another friend who had perished.

"Listen, I can tell you right now that I don't know anything about this Allen guy or what he owes you. Neither does she. We've never met the man before," Sarah said, while nodding at Mandy. "You're wasting your time if that's what you're after."

Samuel grinned, then placed his arms behind his back. A smirk formed on his face as he paced about the floor before her. "I have no doubt that you don't, and to be honest, that's not why you were brought here. We're still tracking Allen down. It's a bit more complicated since the power's out and all, but his debt will be paid in full soon enough."

Madness Rising

"Then why did you kidnap me and my friend?" Sarah asked.

"I'm a business man, Sarah. I operate many streams that generate a nice flow of income. One of those is the facilitator of cash transactions."

"A loan shark, then," Sarah replied with a hint of indignation to her tone.

Samuel nodded, then chuckled. "Basically yes, but the other sounds better."

"It's still illegal either way you slice it," Sarah said.

"Aside from being a loan shark," Samuel said, while pointing at Sarah, "I also provide clients with female companionship. It's a lucrative business that has made me a fairly wealthy man. The demand for young women around the globe is much higher than one might think. You'd be surprised how much my clients are willing to spend on beautiful American women."

A human trafficker. One of the lowest forms a criminal could sink to in her eyes. Tearing innocent girls from their families or preying on those who were lost and helpless made her mad and sick to her stomach. Still, she didn't understand why she and Mandy were there since they were neither of those.

Sarah glanced around to the men that stood at Samuel's back. Each looked at her with stone-cold gazes that made her skin crawl. "So, what? Now you're moving on to grown women? Is that it?"

"Not exactly," Samuel answered. Another man materialized to his right. It was Man-bun. "See, about a year ago, your daughter, Jess, was marked by my crew. Vin here was tasked with procuring her for a buyer we had lined up. Needless to say, things didn't go as planned."

Sarah's eyes swelled with tears as she balled her hands into fists. She cut her gaze over to Man-bun who looked at her with an emotionless stare.

"It's because of you that my baby girl is dead!" Sarah wanted to strangle both men with her bare hands, watching the life drain from their faces. That would be a good start among the other numerous violent acts that swam in her head.

Her butt lifted from the chair. A restrictive hand grabbed her shoulder, and shoved her down. Sarah jerked her shoulder away in anger, but the hand remained.

Mandy wrenched her arms that were tied behind the chair. The gunman moved in and stood close behind her.

"I know how upset you must be, Sarah, but your daughter's death is not what we intended to happen. We had to move sooner than we anticipated, so we improvised," Samuel said.

Sarah squirmed in the chair. The rage she felt wouldn't allow her to sit still. She only saw red. "So, breaking into my house with me and my husband there was your grand plan to grab my daughter?"

"In a manner of speaking, but like I said, my hand was forced. It was a risk that had to be taken. Get inside, nab your daughter, kill you and your husband, and make it look like a home break-in. We even had a note ready to leave in her room stating that she had run away. Her death did not benefit me in any way, but it did cost me a lot of money."

"Good," Sarah said, feeling some sort of justice.

Samuel nodded. "Yes. I imagine you feel the slightest bit of victory from that given what has been taken from you. But, unfortunately for you and your friend, things have taken a rather unique turn. See, the individual who was set to acquire your daughter has agreed to take you and well, now your friend, in lieu of your dead daughter. Having you and your husband, which we haven't been able to locate as of yet, as loose ends with this ugly matter, simply cannot go on any longer."

Sarah scoffed. "Why wait a year? Why didn't you just kill us sooner?"

A radio crackled from one of the goons behind Samuel. The armed gunman pulled it free of his belt and handed it to Samuel.

Samuel held it close to his ear and listened, then nodded at the gunman. "Go sweep the perimeter. Take three guys with you. We might have some company."

The gunman tilted his head and grabbed the radio from Samuel. He pointed at three of the other men. They flanked the man and vanished beyond the large wooden crates.

Vin stood near Samuel with Philip behind Sarah and one other gunman flanking Mandy.

"Simply put, heat from the authorities," Samuel answered. "We know you have friends in the Boston Police Department, and well, they were getting closer than we liked. When the power and communications went down, and the city spiraled into chaos, we seized the opportunity. Nothing like an apocalypse to aid in our endeavors."

Sarah glanced to Mandy who had shiny eyes. A fearful look washed over her face as she fought to speak through the rag shoved in her mouth. Despite the rage that boiled in the pit of Sarah's stomach, they were trapped with no way out. As much as she wanted to bolt from the chair and kill Samuel, she wouldn't make it far. The thought of him not being punished for taking her daughter was worse than the fate that awaited her.

Vin leaned in close, and spoke into Samuel's ear as reports of gunfire popped off from outside of the warehouse.

Samuel recoiled from the sound as he looked about the space. A strained voice barked from the gunman's radio who was behind Mandy.

"We've got company. Multiple—"

The hammering of automatic gunfire screamed from the speaker for a split second, then static.

"Shit," Samuel said. He pointed to Philip. "Take Tommy and go—"

White flashes of muzzle fire flashed from Sarah's left. Gunfire echoed inside the warehouse. Samuel ducked and covered his head as both of his men turned and opened fire.

Sarah dropped to the floor as bullets zipped overhead. Mandy rocked her chair from side to side, tipping it over onto the ground. Her arms were still tied to the bars that connected the front and back legs. She tugged and pulled, trying to set herself free.

"Where the hell are you going?" Samuel asked Vin who was exiting the fight.

Vin took cover behind a tower of boxes. Bullets tore through the edges of the cardboard as he drifted away. "You paid me to find and bring those two here, not engage in a fire fight."

Samuel cowered behind a crate, then pulled a pistol from behind his back. He pointed a rigid finger at Vin. "You've still got one mark left on your contract. Don't forget that or think about screwing me over."

"You worry about yourself, and leave her husband to me. I'll make good on our deal." Vin vanished around the backside of the boxes.

Sarah crawled on her stomach toward Mandy who was slumped over on her side. Mandy flinched with each report. Her chin pressed to her chest as Sarah tapped her shoulder.

"Are you ok?" Sarah asked as she removed the gag from her mouth.

Madness Rising

Mandy nodded while spitting any lose fibers from her lips. "Yeah. What are we going to do?"

The gunman near Mandy took multiple rounds to the chest that punched through his back. He stumbled backward into the stack of crates and crumpled. Blood smeared the face of the wooden boxes and ran down to the floor.

Sarah turned and looked at Samuel who was returning fire to the unknown threat closing in on them.

"I'm going to untie you, then we'll sneak out of here," Sarah said.

The gunfire ebbed.

Samuel snarled. "They're going to pay for this. Mark my words."

He ejected his spent magazine, then pulled a fresh one from his back pocket. He slapped it into place, then cycled a round.

Philip sagged to the side while holding his right shoulder. Blood raced down his thick arm from his shoulder.

Samuel snatched Sarah by her hair and yanked her off the floor. Pain lanced through her head as she grit her teeth. "Untie her friend, and let's go. I'm not losing another big payday here."

Philip bowed and stumbled toward Mandy. He loosened the knot and pulled the rope from her hands.

Sarah kicked at Samuel and swung her balled fists at his arm, trying to break free of his grip. "Let me go."

"Shut it." he said, dragging her through a maze of boxes. "If you two weren't worth so much money to me, I would have already placed a slug in both of your heads."

Samuel navigated the maze at a good clip with Philip and Mandy flanking them. He paused at any open spaces, then skimmed over the area with his pistol up in front of him.

The Irish mobster led them through the remainder of the warehouse to an exit on the far side of the building. Philip grunted and wheezed, but kept moving with Mandy's clothing clutched in his hand.

"You know, you're not going to get away with this, right?" Sarah asked, her voice filled with anger.

Samuel held them up just shy of the door. He leaned in close and pressed the side of his head to the surface. "I hate to break it to you, but I already have. Once you two are gone and your husband is dead, then this will be finished, and I'll move on to the next job."

He rammed the push bar with his hip. The door broke away from the jamb and swung outward. The smoky-gray sky met their eyes as they ran outside.

Philip shoved Mandy out of the building. She stumbled to the ground. Sarah turned to help her to her feet, but Samuel wouldn't give any slack. He wrenched his arm, keeping her close.

Gunfire from inside the warehouse echoed through the open door as Philip lurched. Blood exploded from his chest. The hulking brute collapsed on top of Mandy as she was getting to her feet.

"Screw this. The client wanted you anyway." Samuel left Mandy behind as she fought to crawl out from under Phillip's dead weight.

Sarah reached out for her friend as Samuel dragged her away. She jerked her arm, and pulled toward Mandy.

Samuel kept a tight grip and yanked on her limb.

They moved along the edge of the dock. The waves crashed against the peer below. A multitude of feelings swelled inside of Sarah. Hate, pain, sadness, and fear all slammed into her at once. She had to make him pay for what he had stolen from her and Russell.

Madness Rising

Sarah rammed her elbow into his side. The sharp blow doubled him over, but didn't take him down. She jerked her hair free of his hold.

Samuel shoved her to the ground, then trained his pistol at her chest. A scowl washed over his face as he narrowed his eyes at her.

Multiple gunshots popped off to her left. Samuel flinched, then ducked. He returned fire, squeezing the trigger until the magazine went dry,

Two rounds caught him in the shoulder and chest. The pistol dropped from his hand as he stumbled backward. He dumped over the side of the pier to the water below.

A masked man rushed Sarah, sweeping the area with his piece. He closed in fast and grabbed her by the arm. He yanked her from the ground to her feet.

Sarah shoved him in the chest, then backed away. She looked to the ground for the pistol, then flitted her gaze back to the mysterious man.

He trained his piece at her head, stopping her cold. The whites of his eyes stared at her from the concealment of his dark mask.

Sarah raised her arms in the air, then froze. She narrowed her eyes and pursed her lips. Her brain worked to figure a way out of her predicament.

"Who are you?" she asked, demanding some sort of answer. "Why did you help me, and what's going on here?"

The masked man looked to the opening of the warehouse, then back to Sarah. His hand repositioned over the grip of his piece. "We need to move. Now."

His voice was deep, raspy, yet it sounded vaguely familiar, one that she struggled to place in that heated moment of tension and stress.

A thought flourished inside her head as to the mysterious man's identity. It made her more nervous and scared than what she already was. Although she wasn't one hundred percent sure, her gut feeling begged her to listen.

Sarah swallowed the lump of fear that clogged her throat, then asked, "Spencer? Is that, you?"

Madness Rising

CHAPTER TWENTY-THREE

RUSSELL

The rucksack weighed heavily on Russell's back. A dull, nagging pain tormented his muscles. Each step over the rugged terrain punished his body. His shoulders sagged with exhaustion and his legs burned, but he couldn't stop.

Johnson lifted his arm in the air, then balled his fingers into a fist. He stooped down and groaned, within the tall blades of grass and bushes with his attention trained ahead.

Russell crouched and moved to his side with both dogs flanking him. They stayed silent, but remained on high alert. Their ears stood on end as they waited for their handler's command.

"That's it," Johnson said. His face contorted in pain as he pointed to a large, sheet-metal building. "Best guess, this is where he'd bring her. It's far enough away from any prying eyes. Plus, it's secluded. Surrounded by trees for miles."

Madness Rising

Russell skimmed over the area for any movement. The outside was void of any armed gunmen. Rows of eighteen wheelers lined the far side of the structure. Heaps of timber littered the open yard. A mixture of trucks and SUV's were parked in front of what appeared to be the entrance to the building. There didn't appear to be any work going on, but that didn't mean there wasn't any activity on the inside.

"I don't see any of his men stationed outside," Russell said. "From the way Tony spoke, he made it sound like they'd be on high alert."

"Who knows," Johnson shot back. "Those radios only work so far before they become choppy. Plus, with communications being down, that could be affecting it as well. Besides, having a bunch of men standing around a building with rifles and what not looks suspicious at best."

Russell pulled the radio from his hip and switched it on. Static hissed from the speaker as he thumbed through the different channels. "I've got nothing here. If they're in there, they're being awfully quiet."

Johnson shrugged. "I don't know what to tell you. This is my best guess."

Russell switched the radio off, then ran his hand over his face. He glanced at the building and sighed. "All right. We go down there, and check it out, then."

"We?" Johnson asked with a raised brow. "I brought you here which has already put me at risk. I'm not stepping foot into that building or anywhere around it. This is as far as I go. Plus, my leg is messed up."

"Oh, but I think you are. You're not done yet." Russell stood, then jerked Johnson from the ground by the scruff of his uniform.

"All right, damn." Johnson hissed as he favored his injured leg.

Both Max and Butch sprung from their crouched positions.

"Is there another way inside the building besides the main entrance or roll up doors?" Russell asked.

Johnson pointed to the east side of the building. "Yeah. There's an entrance over there we can use."

Russell ejected the magazine from his pistol and looked it over. He only had maybe three or four rounds left. "Do you have any magazines left on your duty belt?"

"Yeah. I've got one left." Johnson removed it from its pouch and gave it up.

Russell secured the additional magazine in his back pocket. He moved out of the tree line and down the hill with Max and Butch flanking him. Johnson limped along at his side as they made their way to the open yard.

They used the large heaps of scraped timber as cover and darted from one mound to the other. Butch and Max sniffed the dirt and sawdust that carpeted the ground.

The dogs worked their way through a narrow gap between two large piles of stacked wood toward the building. Russell followed close behind as Johnson brought up the rear.

"Hold up, guys," Russell said, in a low tone as they neared the edge of the massive tree trunks. He squeezed past the dogs, then peered out into the open space which was free and clear of any threats. "All right. Let's go."

Russell took the lead with Max and Butch at his side. Johnson grumbled under his breath, but moved just the same.

The east side of the building had more stacks of discarded lumber that littered the grounds. It made it hard to spot any threats within the jumbled mess. Russell relied on the dogs who didn't offer any warnings.

Madness Rising

They navigated the maze which led to a single steel door that was propped open. Russell brought the pistol to bear and approached with caution. Smoke plumed from inside and lifted into the air.

Chatter could be heard from the opening. Russell paused, then tilted his head. He couldn't make out what was being said as their voices were muffled and faint.

The door pushed open a hair farther. Russell froze, then drew a sharp breath. Both Max and Butch lowered their ears as subtle growls called from their throats.

A hand emerged from the building, then flicked an extinguished cigarette bud to the ground. Boisterous laughter rang out as the door slammed shut.

Russell advanced, stopping shy of the door. He glanced back to Johnson.

"You know you're going to get us killed, Cage," Johnson said, in a low whisper. "This is nothing short of suicide."

"I'm not, so shut up," Russell replied.

He leaned in close and pressed his ear to the door. He couldn't detect any chatter or other sounds from the other side. Perhaps they moved on. It was a risk worth taking.

Russell grabbed the silver handle mounted near the edge of the door. Max stood at the ready by his side with his nose trained at the opening. Butch growled as he waited patiently to move.

Russell gently tugged on the handle. The door opened without resistance. The hinges squeaked, but it was subtle and barely audible. He froze and listened for any responses to the noise just the same. None came.

Max inched closer to the narrow gap. His nose tested the air as Russell opened the door more. He motioned with his hand for the German shepherd to stay put. Max stepped back as Russell pulled open the door.

He peered inside the dimly lit space. Shadows plagued the area and made it hard to see. He didn't spot any figures moving within the murk or hear any footfalls to indicate that danger was close at hand.

"Ok. Give me the lay-" Russell said, as he glanced back. Johnson was no longer there. Russell craned his neck and searched for the deputy, but couldn't lay eyes on him.

Damnit.

Russell pursed his lips and cursed under his breath. He wasn't surprised by the deputy leaving him high and dry. His treachery was bound to happen sooner or later. Russell just hoped he ran away, and didn't decide to alert anyone to their presence. Given his reluctance to come this close, Russell figured he tucked tail and bolted.

It was heads or tails of where to start, so Russell decided to head up the stairs. Perhaps he'd be able to get a better view of the building from up high.

The dogs funneled inside and sniffed the ground as Russell closed the door. The outer edges kissed the jamb, but didn't sound a warning.

Russell patted his leg and headed up the stairs. Both Max and Butch followed close behind. The soles of his boots clanged off each step as they climbed to the catwalk.

The murk faded away to strident light that shone through massive windows that rimmed the backside of the building. Russell trained the barrel at the steel walkway with his back against the railing.

They hit the landing and moved along the catwalk. Offices lined the south side of the walkway, starting about twelve feet before them. The interiors of each were dark and absent of any movement.

Russell glanced over the side of the railing and spotted two men standing near one of the roll up doors. Each had rifles slung over their shoulders as they chatted. There was no sign of Cathy, but the building was big, and the main entrance was on the far side.

They continued on, moving past each office as Russell glanced through the dingy windows. He skimmed over the dark interior, finding nothing more than vacant desks and empty bookcases.

Butch growled, then turned around to face the way they came. The muscles in his back and shoulders twitched as he lowered his head. Footfalls echoed up the steel steps toward the catwalk.

Russell glanced to the office they were close by, then back to the stairs. He didn't want to get into a shoot-out. Stealth and silence were their best chance at finding Cathy undetected.

He opened the door to the office and funneled the dogs inside just as one of Marcus's men hit the landing. The man stopped, then lit a cigarette as Russell dipped inside the stale smelling space. He pushed the door closed and peered out of the small, square window next to the entrance.

The man came into view as he strolled down the walkway. Smoke seeped through his lips as his hand rested on the grip of the pistol nestled in the front part of his jeans. It didn't appear as if he was in search of any sort of threat, but he appeared to be ready if he found one.

The canines grew anxious, moaning and growling from the footfalls that drew closer. Russell shushed them again, but it did little good. The threat beyond the walls had them on edge, and they were struggling to contain themselves.

"Guys. You need to keep it—"

Butch barked.

Russell cringed, then peered out through the blinds.

The man stopped, then yanked the pistol from his jeans. The cigarette was fixed between his lips as he sucked on the end. He turned toward the empty office before the one they were in. He brought his weapon to bear and inched toward the space.

Russell watched him scope out the office, then vanish from sight. He craned his neck as far as he could and waited for him to come back into view.

The man shut the door, then continued on. Russell closed the blinds and ducked. He moved to the side of the entrance of the office, and crouched against the wall as he kept watch on the door. Butch groaned, but stayed silent. Max stood at the ready at Russell's side.

The doorknob twisted.

The canines' growling grew louder and more intense.

Russell gulped, then drew a sharp breath as his finger slipped over the trigger.

The door cracked open. A thin beam of light bled into the office. Russell tilted the barrel of the pistol upward, ready to fire if need be. He had no intentions of killing the man unless absolutely necessary. He probably knew where they were keeping Cathy.

The hinges squeaked as the man pushed the door open farther. His arms came into view as he stepped forward.

Russell grabbed his wrist and jumped up. The barrel of his pistol pressed to the man's temple before he could think of chambering off a single round.

"Don't even think about pulling that trigger," Russell said.

"Who the hell are you?" the man asked.

Russell pried the weapon from the man's hand and secured it behind his back. "It's none of your concern who I am. Where are you keeping the woman?"

"What woman?" the man asked.

"Don't mess with me, pal." Russell grabbed a handful of the man's shirt and shoved him against the door. "The woman your boss kidnapped. Where are they keeping her?"

Madness Rising

The man held his hands in the air in protest, then said, "Listen, I don't know—"

Russell pressed the barrel into the middle of the man's forehead. Max and Butch growled as they stalked the man from the shadows.

"I'd rather not kill you, but if you don't tell me what I want to know, I will," Russell said. "Now, where is she?"

"All right, man, just calm down and lower that canon," the man said, with a stutter. "She's over on the far side. One of the offices. Room 2B."

Russell lowered the weapon from the man's head to his torso. "How many men are in the building?"

"Four including me. The place is shut down since the power's out."

A knocking noise from down the walkway caught Russell's attention. He peered out of the office, and around the jamb of the door while keeping his piece trained on Marcus's lackey.

The man slapped his arm away, then shoved him backward. Russell lost his balance, and fell to the floor as the man bolted from the office. Both Max and Butch chased after him.

"No, no, no," Russell said, as he pulled himself off the floor.

He rushed out of the office and ran after Butch and Max. They raced across the catwalk at full tilt. There was still a chance to get to the man before he warned everyone else that they were here.

The man rushed down a small set of steps and kept running across the metal gangway. He peered over his shoulder at the dogs.

Russell struggled to keep pace with the galloping canines. He wheezed, and struggled to catch his breath, but pushed on. His hand glided along the railing as he labored down the set of small steps.

The man trampled down a set of stairs that led to the ground below. Max and Butch kept with him stride for stride as they vanished from Russell's sight.

Things had gone from bad to worse in a blink. Russell was out of his element and treading water that was trying to overtake him.

His boots hammered each step as he flew down the staircase. He swept the area with his pistol, but couldn't lay eyes on the dogs or any of Marcus's men for that matter.

Russell's chest heaved, and his lungs begged for air. He panted as he licked his dry, cracked lips. Sweat populated his brow and trickled down the sides of his face.

He worked his way through the machinery on the ground floor toward the double doors that led to the main entrance of the building. An array of large saws and conveyer belts with trees strapped to them took up much of the space. It was a maze of steel that had too many places for Marcus's men to hide.

Faint barks from the dogs echoed throughout the space, and made him pause. He listened, but couldn't pinpoint where it was coming from.

Gunfire made Russell flinch. He ducked and searched for the source. He dropped to the ground and scrambled for cover.

The contents in the rucksack shifted about as he ducked behind a stack of wooden pallets. He deflated against the edge and exhaled. He looked for the shooter through the narrow gaps of the machinery, but couldn't lay eyes on him.

Another round popped off, striking the outside of the wood near his head. Russell retreated to the far side and got to his feet. A set of boots came into view as he collided with the burly man.

Russell squeezed the trigger on impulse without aiming. The bullet went wide by a mile.

Madness Rising

The burly man knocked the pistol from his hand, then punched Russell in the face. The blow rocked him, but didn't take him down. His face pulsated and ached as tears blurred his vision. The man's hand felt like cinderblocks.

Russell shook his head, then squinted as the burly man reached for his pistol. He pulled the weapon from the saw dust on the ground and brought it to bear.

Max leapt from the conveyer belt next to them and latched onto the man's arm. Fire spat from the muzzle as Max jerked the man to the ground. The single round kicked up dirt next to Russell's feet. He jumped and backed away.

Screams fled the man's bearded mouth as Max thrashed his head from side to side.

Russell caught movement out of the corner of his eye. Another one of Marcus's men had gotten the drop on him. The short, stocky man shouldered his rifle and lined up his shot with Russell's head.

Russell lifted his arms into the air, surrendering.

Butch stalked the man from behind, panting heavily.

The man froze as his eyes went wide. He wrenched the rifle about. The cane corso lunged and tackled him with ease. He mounted the frightened man as he tried to scoot away.

Butch snapped at any part of the man's body he could latch onto. Terrified screams of panic fled the man's mouth as he pushed at the dog's neck. Butch latched onto his wrist and jerked his head until the man stopped fighting back.

"Mr. Cage," a voice said, nearby. "Russell Cage, why don't you come out, and let's chat?"

Russell didn't recognize the voice, but figured it had to be Marcus.

219

Derek Shupert

"Max, come on," Russell said, making his way past the stack of pallets.

Max let go of the burly man's arm and followed at his side. They halted at the edge of the pallets as Russell scoped out the area. He couldn't see the man who called for him and didn't want to risk venturing out into the open and catching a bullet to the head.

"Who's wanting to chat?" Russell asked.

"I think you know who," the smug voice replied. "I've got our mutual lady friend here."

"How do I know you're not going to shoot me in the head when I step out into the open?"

"You don't, but seeing as you're shit up a creek without a paddle, I guess you're going to have to trust me."

Russell pulled his shirt over the pistol, then stepped out from his cover with his arms in the air. Cathy stood just beyond the double doors with a man crouched behind her. Her blonde hair was a tattered mess, her face was smirched with dirt, and she had a cut above her right brow.

Marcus eyed Russell from over her shoulder, then pointed his gun in their direction. "Now those are some vicious animals. Make sure you keep them inline. I'd hate to have to put them down."

Russell couldn't get a clear view of the man's face or any part of his body.

"You ok?" Russell asked as he walked toward them. Both Max and Butch flanked him on either side, growling and baring their fangs.

"Yeah. I'm all right," Cathy answered in a weak voice. She looked to Max who groaned and whined. He took a step toward her.

Russell halted him with his hand. He stayed put, for now.

Marcus had two of his men off to either side of him. Both had rifles shouldered and trained in Russell's direction.

220

Madness Rising

"You know, for some city slicker from Boston, you sure are full of surprises," Marcus said, in a raised voice. "That rat Deputy Johnson, who we caught outside of the building and who is now dead, told me about you. If he would have done his job and snuffed you while he had the chance, that would've made my world a billion times easier. But instead, he brought you all the way to my front door, and now, I have to clean up his mess."

Russell wasn't a fan of Johnson, but he didn't want to see him die. In the end, though, he'd reaped what he'd sowed.

"The sheriff knows all about what you've done. You do anything to either of us, and you'll be in a world of hurt," Russell replied.

"And who exactly is going to care about either of you?" Marcus asked. "I own this town. Every single resident is pressed under my thumb, and most wouldn't dare cross me. Well, except for Ms. Cathy here. She's been a pain in my side for some time. Because of her stubborn nature and lack of reasoning, some of the other town's people have started to push back, questioning how I do things. This has complicated my business and forced me to escalate matters. I could just kill her and take her property, but she'd be much more valuable to me as an asset. If I can have her tout a change of heart toward me and how wonderful I am, then perhaps other folks will take notice. That, and she's easy on the eyes, wouldn't you say?"

The double doors swung outward as a figure loomed in the shadows of the hallway.

"Look at that. The cavalry is here," Marcus said, in a mocking tone. "Looks like I'm in trouble now."

Sheriff Donner strolled out into the open and walked past Cathy and Marcus. He turned to the side and stopped halfway between Russell and them.

"I knew you were on his payroll," Cathy said, as she thrashed in Marcus's embrace. "You're going to end up the same way as your deputy. Dead."

Donner's emotionless gaze lingered on Cathy. His hands rested on his duty belt. He didn't respond to her violent outburst, but instead, looked at Marcus.

"I'm glad you're here, Sheriff," Marcus said, as he held onto Cathy's body. "I'd like to report a trespasser on my property. Do you think you can take care of that for me?"

Sheriff Donner looked to Russell. His hand shifted to the Glock on his hip. "Yeah. I'll take care of him. Have your men lower their rifles, though. I don't want any itchy trigger fingers accidently shooting me today."

"You heard the sheriff, boys. Go ahead and lower your weapons."

Marcus's men lowered their rifles and held them close to their chests. They stood in place and watched as the sheriff removed his Glock from his holster.

Donner clutched the piece in his hand with his finger over the trigger. He peered down at the Glock, and stared at it for a few seconds.

"Everything all right, Sheriff?" Marcus asked. "I'd like to get this wrapped up as fast as possible."

"Actually, no, everything is not all right," Donner replied with a heavy sigh.

He turned toward Marcus and brought his Glock to bear. He fired at the henchmen flanking Marcus. Both men dropped to the ground before they could shoulder their rifles.

"What the hell," Marcus said, in disbelief. He pulled the pistol away from Cathy's head and fired.

Fire spat from the end of the weapon. Two rounds impacted with the sheriff's chest and knocked him to the ground.

Madness Rising

Cathy stomped Marcus's foot with the heel of her boot, then rammed her elbow into his face. His head snapped back. She pulled away from his arms.

Max took off running and made a beeline toward him.

"You bitch," Marcus said, as blood trickled from his nose. "You're going to pay for that."

He lined the barrel of his pistol up with the small of her back as Max raced to stop him.

Russell pulled the weapon from behind his back and opened fire. He squeezed the trigger until it clicked empty. Multiple rounds punched through Marcus's chest. The pistol fell from Marcus's hand as he crumbled to the ground.

Max diverted his attention to Cathy who was on her side. He licked at her face as she wrapped her arms around his neck and hugged him.

Sheriff Donner laid prone on his back, coughing and hacking up blood. He'd been hit in the chest and side. Blood smirched his uniform.

Russell approached with caution as Butch growled at his side. He kicked the sheriff's firearm away and trained his piece at his chest.

"Did you grow a conscience?" Russell asked.

"Yeah. Something like that," Donner said, as he grimaced in pain. "I should have stopped this years ago. All of this and everything else that's happened is all my fault."

Cathy stood up and walked over to the sheriff with Max at her side. She glanced over the wounds, then said, "Those look severe. Not sure we could get him to the hospital before he bleeds out."

Donner dismissed the notion with a wave of his hand. "Don't worry about me. You two need to get out of here."

223

"How do we know we can trust him to take care of it?" Russell said. "His deputy and former boss threatened my wife and tried to kill us while he did nothing to stop it."

"I have a lot of wrong to make up for. Let me handle this. Besides, I'll probably bleed out before too long," Donner replied in a weak tone.

Russell wasn't keen on having to finish off the sheriff, despite what he had done. The other men he had shot were in self-defense and to preserve his and Cathy's life.

He lowered the pistol as Donner nodded toward the double doors. His trembling hand reached for the radio on his shoulder.

"Go. Get out of here."

Cathy and Russell stared at one another as Donner spoke into his radio. Static crackled from the speaker as he paused, then kept going. It was unclear if he was getting through or not.

"Come on, Butch," Russell said, as they fled the scene.

They worked their way through the dark, abandoned office and out through the front doors. Russell skimmed over the two trucks and SUV that were parked in front of the main entrance. He made for the red Bronco.

The dogs were loaded through the rear of the vehicle. Russell removed the rucksack from his back and shoved it across the black, leather bench seat. He settled into the driver's seat and shut his door.

Cathy slammed the rear hatch, then ran to the passenger side door. She scaled the side of the SUV and hopped inside.

Russell reached for the keys in the ignition, but they weren't there. He looked about aimless, unsure of where to check.

"Here." Cathy grabbed the driver's side visor and pulled down. A set of keys dropped into Russell's lap.

"Really?" he said.

Cathy shrugged. "People are simple and trusting in the mountains."

Madness Rising

Russell shook his head, then fired up the engine. The Bronco started without fault. He pumped the gas, revving the engine.

Russell shifted into reverse and backed away from the building. He spun the steering wheel counterclockwise, pumped the brake, then shifted into drive.

The back tires tore into the ground, slinging clumps of dirt and chunks of rock from under the thick tread as they drove away from the lumber mill.

They hit the dirt that wound down through the hills, leaving the nightmare they faced behind them.

CHAPTER TWENTY-FOUR

RUSSELL

The ride back to Luray was an uneventful drive. Russell checked the rearview mirror for any inbound trucks, but none came. Dirt morphed to pavement as they booked it down the highway.

Max licked at Cathy's face. He whined and nearly crawled over the front seat to be with her. Butch sat on his haunches, staring out of the backseat window with his stern, focused gaze.

"Yeah. I'm happy to see you too." Cathy's voice was jovial. A warm smile slid across her face as she hugged and kissed Max's head. "All right, sit back."

Max gave his thick coat a shake, then sat down.

"That's one happy pup," Russell said. "He missed you a lot."

"Not as much as I missed him. Thanks for looking out for him. Don't know what I would do without him," Cathy responded as she rubbed his head. "Same with this guy."

Butch looked her way, then licked at her fingers.

A look of dread instantly washed over her face as she stared at Russell. "Oh God. Thomas. Is he ok?"

"I'm not sure, to be honest. After the sheriff got on the scene, he dragged me down to the station. He said he was going to have Thomas taken to the hospital. I figure we'll stop by there real quick, check on him, and drop Butch off before we head out."

"I hope he's all right. He's a good man. Been like a father to me," Cathy said, in a somber tone.

"I think he'll be fine. He seems like a tough old bastard."

"Yeah. That he is." Cathy cleared her throat. "Thanks for coming to get me and all that. Aside from Thomas, I don't have many people I consider friends around these parts. I mean, you could have bailed, but I'm glad you didn't. So, yeah. Thanks."

Russell teetered on the brink of coming clean that he considered leaving, but decided against it. There was no need to tell her that. Instead, he nodded. "You saved my ass. I returned the favor. Consider us square."

Cathy smirked. "Yeah. We're square."

The roads were null of any traffic, allowing Cathy and Russell to make good time.

They arrived back in town and stopped at the local hospital. Max was kept in the back of the Bronco while Butch was let out. The entrance to the hospital was dark. The automatic sliding glass doors were propped open far enough for people to pass through.

The waiting room was empty except for four people sitting in the far seats. Nurses and other medical staff scurried about with clipboards and charts clutched in their hands.

"Excuse me, ma'am," Russell said, to the nurse behind the front counter.

She looked up from her chart. "Yes. How may I help you?"

"Hi. Yes, we're looking for a-"

Butch barked, then spun around in circles.

"Hey, you can't have that dog in here. This is a hospital, not an animal shelter," she said, while leaning toward the counter.

Butch didn't pay her any mind as he darted past Russell and Cathy. The cane corso galloped across the lobby toward a man in a wheel chair.

The nurse stormed around the counter in a huff, searching for the large, black beast.

Thomas rolled through the lobby as Butch lowered his head and wagged his tail. "There's my big boy."

Butch licked at Thomas's fingers, then jumped up into his lap.

"Sir, that dog can't be-"

Russell tapped the nurse on the shoulder. "Give the guy a break. He was in an accident, and that dog is his world. It's not like they're roaming through the hospital. We're just in the lobby."

"Oh really. Well, thank you for letting me know that," the nurse replied tersely. She looked to Thomas, then back to Russell. "That animal doesn't go any farther."

Russell nodded. "Yes, ma'am."

Cathy shrugged as Thomas wheeled up to them with Butch at his side.

"Aren't you two a sight for sore eyes," he said, with a smile. "You both look like hammered crap, but I'm happy to see that you're ok."

Cathy hugged his neck. "How are you doing?"

Madness Rising

Thomas rubbed Butch's head, then said, "I'm good. Sore and banged up some, but I'll live. It'll take a bit more than a car wreck to keep me down."

Russell patted Thomas's shoulder and smiled. "We're just glad you're ok. That's all that matters."

"Yeah. You and me both," Thomas replied. "So, what happened with Marcus? Didn't you tell the sheriff and get it straightened out?"

Cathy and Russell looked at each other, then nodded.

"Yeah. It's been handled. Don't think we'll have to worry about him bothering us anymore," Cathy said.

"That's great news," Thomas replied. "So, I take it you'll be heading out now?"

"Yeah. We need to get on the road," Cathy answered. "I can stay if you need me to."

Thomas dismissed the offer with a wave of his hand. "Not at all. You go to your daughter, and get this man to his wife. Me and Butch will be fine."

"You sure?" Cathy asked.

"I am. I'll sweet talk Ms. Nurse-lady over there about Butch as we get things wrapped up here." Thomas winked, then smiled.

Cathy gave him one last hug. "Thank you for everything, and sorry about all of the trouble."

"Not a problem, sweetie. That's what family is for."

Butch groaned and nudged her hand. She dropped to a knee and rubbed the sides of his head.

"Thanks again for everything, sir. It's much appreciated," Russell said, while extending his hand.

Thomas grabbed hold and gave him a firm handshake. "You're welcome, son. Get back to that wife of yours."

"Will do, sir."

Russell knelt before Butch. His hand rubbed under his maw as the cane corso licked his face. Russell didn't lean away or complain. Instead, he took the loving gesture and embraced the beast's neck. "You take care of him, all right?"

Butch groaned and gave Russell one last lick before he stood up.

"Looks like you got some bonding time in," Thomas observed.

"That we did," Russell said.

"If you need a ride, I still got my other vehicle," Thomas said. "It should be good to go."

Cathy glanced to the entrance. "Thanks, but we found one. Besides, your SUV is toast, and you'll need it."

"Good deal. I'm glad you found a ride. Give Amber my best."

"I will." Cathy gave Thomas one last hug before walking away.

Russell shook his hand and nodded.

They headed out of the hospital to the Bronco where Max was looking out the cracked window. He pawed at the glass and paced about the backseat as they loaded up into the SUV. The German shepherd licked the side of Russell's face as he started the vehicle up.

"We ready to do this?" Russell asked.

Cathy nodded. "Philadelphia, here we come."

Madness Rising

Derek Shupert

ABOUT THE AUTHOR

Derek Shupert is an emerging Science Fiction Author known for his captivating dystopian storylines and post-apocalyptic-laden plots. With various books and anthologies underway, he is also the author of the Afflicted series and Sentry Squad.

Outside of the fantastical world of sci-fi, Derek serves as the Vice President at Woodforest National Bank. During his free time, he enjoys reading, exercising, and watching apocalyptic movies and TV shows like Mad Max and The Walking Dead. Above all, he is a family man who cherishes nothing more than quality time spent with his loved ones.

To find out more about Derek Shupert and his forthcoming publications, visit his official website at **www.derekshupert.com.**

Made in the USA
Las Vegas, NV
18 May 2024

90033012R00142